THE MAN
FROM U.N.C.L.E. No. 8

The Mad Scientist Affair

THE MAN FROM U.N.C.L.E. No. 8

The Mad Scientist Affair

JOHN T. PHILLIFENT

Based on the MGM television series
The Man from U.N.C.L.E.

Published by Souvenir Press Ltd.
in association with
The New English Library Ltd.

First published in Great Britain by Souvenir Press Ltd.,
95 Mortimer Street, London, W.1, in association with
The New English Library Ltd., Barnard's Inn, Holborn, London, E.C.1,
in October 1966

*Four Square Books are published by The New English Library Limited, from Barnard's
Inn, Holborn, London, E.C.1. Made and printed in Great Britain by
Cox & Wyman Ltd., London, Reading and Fakenham.*

THE MAD SCIENTIST AFFAIR

PROLOGUE

JULY was dying in a blaze of sub-tropical swelter, and New York was one vast oven as the two men marched side by side along to Del Floria's tailor shop. They were looking forward to air-conditioned comfort for a brief while, at least, inside.

An uninformed onlooker would have seen only a row of aged and unremarkable brownstones, with one fairly new three-storied whitestone at the south end of the row to lend a little tone, but these two men knew that the exterior belied the facts. They knew, for instance, just how exclusive was the key-club restaurant, *The Masked Club*, which took up the first and second floors of the whitestone. They knew that the innocent and rather ordinary offices on the third floor, an organization calling itself U.N.C.L.E., was a pale shadow of the reality. Under that façade of crumbling stone, decrepit shops, a struggling garage and a clutter of lower-income residents, there was one large and complex modern building, the headquarters of the real U.N.C.L.E.

There, in a maze of steel-walled corridors and ultra-modern suites, an extremely efficient squad of brisk and alert young people of all nations and persuasions made it their unrelenting business to be curious about, and deal with, anything at all that offered a threat to international law and order. They had on call every resource of modern technology, plus the drive that comes from hard training and utter dedication.

The two men now passing through the secret entrance in the tailor shop knew as much about it as anyone and more than most. One was Napoleon Solo, Chief Enforcement Agent for U.N.C.L.E., and the other was that imperturbable and coldly efficient technologist and gatherer of unusual and useful information, Illya Nickovetch Kuryakin.

CHAPTER ONE

'ARE YOU DELIBERATELY TRYING TO GIVE ME THE COLD SHIVERS?'

ALEXANDER WAVERLY was in a rare mood as he clutched an unlit pipe and eyed the two agents who had come in response to his summons. The Chief of Section One of U.N.C.L.E. usually looked like an untidy, rather severe professor who was about to pronounce caustic judgment on some miserable student, but at this moment he twinkled. Because of this Solo frowned and felt uneasy.

'It's our business to know what's going on,' Waverly began. 'We must begin with the facts, no matter how fantastic they may seem. Don't be too quick to judge, therefore, as I introduce you to an eccentric genius, one Michael O'Rourke, who lives in a castle in Ireland and calls himself "King" Mike. This is his face.' He swivelled his chair to stare at the screen on the wall as a picture suddenly glowed there. The man in the picture was old, with a halo of white hair and a bristling white beard that came to a caprine point, but he had been caught in a sardonic smile, showing a lively eye.

A female voice recited the dossier of this man over a loudspeaker concealed somewhere in the room:

'Dr. Michael O'Rourke, biochemist, bachelor, age 58. Travelled extensively and adventurously in youth, often on the wrong side of the law. Is now head of chemical research for O'Brien's Beautiful Beers, Inc., at their highly modern brewery near Conway, County Clare, Eire. As well as its commercial functions, the laboratory conducts pure research into vitamins, proteins and molecular chemistry, under Dr. O'Rourke's direction.'

The goat-bearded grin faded and was replaced by a picturesque view of a castle in bright sunshine over a green moor.

1

'Cooraclare Castle,' the impersonal voice went on, 'is small, typical of the region, but of dubious authenticity. Dr. O'Rourke acquired it four years ago, has modernized its interior, and lives there with a small staff and his two nieces, the daughters of his two brothers, now deceased. The nieces assist their uncle in the laboratory. The castle is three miles from the brewery, four miles from Conway. Dr. O'Rourke is known locally as "King" Mike.'

Solo grinned. 'I never yet knew an Irishman who didn't claim to be a descendant of one of the kings of ould Ireland. This one seems to believe it.'

'It's a real castle, at any rate,' Kuryakin murmured. 'The architecture looks genuine. Apart from being a mad scientist, why are we interested in him, sir?'

Waverly stroked his cheek with the stem of his cold pipe. He was very seldom seen to light this up, and he didn't now. 'O'Rourke is, as you say, a mad – or eccentric – scientist. It is not a crime. Nor is it reprehensible to seek to improve the quality of beer. Quite the reverse. I like a glass of O'Brien's myself, on occasion. It's very good. But wait.'

The castle picture gave way to another portrait, this time of a pudgy-faced, timid-looking man with wispy dark hair and eyes which peered trustfully through heavy pebble lenses. The unseen female voice went on:

'Dr. Vittorio Trilli, Genovese biochemist, brilliant but unorthodox. Was in trouble with authorities over illegal experimentation before he was believed to be killed in a mysterious laboratory explosion in Milan, four years ago. Is known to us to be a high-ranking THRUSH field-agent ... and alive.'

Solo nodded grimly. That was a very familiar story.

The voice went on: 'Our man in Limerick reports Trilli is in the neighbourhood and very interested in O'Rourke. Trilli is accompanied by two lesser THRUSH agents – muscle-men.'

Waverly swung his chair around to face Solo and Illya again. '... and there you are,' he said, nursing his pipe and watching his two top agents with some curiosity, trying to guess how their thoughts would run.

2

'That will be THRUSH-ITALIAN,' Solo mused, 'and if you'd ever tasted the Italian version of bottled beer you wouldn't be surprised about their trying to learn some Irish knowhow. Perhaps they want O'Rourke to build a brewery in Rome for them?'

Kuryakin was characteristic in wasting no time on wit; he went for the key points: 'THRUSH believes he's on to something useful. Trilli's there to find out what, and grab it.'

Waverly nodded. 'I would agree. For once, we can let THRUSH do the hard work for us. If O'Rourke *has* developed something, Trilli will validate it for us. He will then try to grab it. That's where we will step in. Until then, however, I think someone should keep a very sharp eye on Trilli.'

'Ireland!' Solo sighed softly. 'County Clare at this time of year should be very pleasant.' He thought of the blistering heat outside and smiled. Very pleasant indeed. But Waverly looked to Kuryakin.

'You' – he pointed his pipe-stem – 'will leave immediately. Fly to Shannon, which is right on the spot where it is all happening. Use your own judgment as to cover. Remember, your job is to let Trilli start something, then see that you finish it. Understood?'

'Isn't that asking rather a lot of just one agent?' Solo asked hopefully.

Waverly swung on him, again aiming his pipe. 'I have something else for you, closer to home. The other end of the thread, perhaps.' He swivelled to the screen again, which now showed a glowing picture of two very lovely faces side by side. The one on the left was Latin-dark and vivid, her heart-shaped face smouldering and exotic – the absolute converse of the girl on the right, who was fair in a roses-and-cream way, with a shy smile, cornflower-blue eyes and masses of heavy golden-blonde hair. Solo stared and promptly forgot all about Irish scenery.

The impassive voice on the loudspeaker continued: 'Bridget and Sarah O'Rourke,' and as the picture gave way to another, that of the shy-smiling blonde girl alone, it went

3

on: 'Sarah O'Rourke, single, age twenty-five, at present in New York, attending a convention of chemists and bio-chemists, to deliver a paper on "Some Aspects of Molecular Structure as Evidenced in New Synthetic Yeasts" later this afternoon.'

Waverly spun his chair again. 'That paper may or may not tell us something,' he commented. 'Undoubtedly the girl herself can. You, Mr. Solo, will see that she does. You will make her acquaintance, gain her confidence, and get her to talk. You should be able to manage that, I imagine?'

Solo dragged his appreciative gaze away from the shy smile and looked down to meet his chief's quizzical stare. He smoothed his face hastily. 'I think I can manage, sir. I gather there's a cover already prepared for me?'

'You'll collect your official invitation and papers on the way out. A room is booked for you. That will be all for now, gentlemen.'

The two turned and marched away. Solo grinned and murmured, 'Better watch yourself with Bridget, Illya. She bears all the earmarks of a real "femme fatale". Not your kind at all.'

'Considering what you know about biochemistry,' Kuryakin retorted with a smile, 'I'm sorry I can't stay to hear you trying to charm Miss Sarah. It ought to be interesting.'

Solo was looking forward to meeting Miss Sarah O'Rourke herself, but not to her biochemistry. Exhaustively thorough training within the U.N.C.L.E. organization had made him able to take care of himself in virtually any situation, but his store of any technical information was necessarily superficial – certainly enough to get by but not enough to fool a professional specialist. He hoped, wryly, that she wouldn't prove to be a fanatic in her own subject. *With a face like that?* he thought, smiling.

The elevator let him out into a buzz of talk and the move-ments of many people, all with lapel-pins giving their names. His own was in place. He drifted, surveying the

4

chattering groups without seeming to do so, making his way to where an easel stood supporting a blackboard decorated with notices. He found the schedule for the day, ran his eye down the listed entries, and there it was. And he stared in sudden suspicion, because someone had run a heavy blue line through Miss S. O'Rourke's name and time, and alongside had scribbled 'Cancelled'.

Stepping back, Solo swept the room with a sharp eye, spotted one man who sported a blue tag against the standard white ones, and approached him, assuming him to be a person of some authority.

'Dr. Mercer? Can you by any chance tell me why Miss O'Rourke's talk—?'

'Ah, tragic. Yes, indeed. Not five minutes ago. Lost her voice all at once. Most peculiar. Psychosomatic, probably. Stage-fright, you know?'

'I see,' Solo murmured, keeping an unchanged expression despite the sudden blaze of suspicion in his mind. From the corner of his eye he caught sight of a face very familiar to him, swung hastily so that his back was to it, and smiled at Mercer. 'It's a bit of a blow. I was particularly interested in—'

'Ah, in that case!' Dr. Mercer did not seem to like anyone to complete a sentence. 'This way, this way.' He led off smartly towards the side of the room. Solo followed, frowning, alert for more of THRUSH's minions. He saw one more, and his first suspicion became certainty. He was convinced Sarah had been clobbered in some way to stop her delivering her paper. He moved warily on Mercer's heels until they reached a long low table strewn with paper. Mercer cast his eye along the piles and reached for one. 'Here you are, Dr. - er - Solo? This is a mimeoed copy of Miss O'Rourke's paper. Your field, I gather?'

'Eh?' Solo took the sheets, snatched at his confused wits and managed to nod and smile. 'Shall we just say I'm interested? Quick work, these papers. I mean, you said it was only five minutes ago that Miss O'Rourke lost her voice, didn't you?'

'These were run off this morning.' Mercer lost a little

5

of his ready geniality. 'It's the usual thing, you know, where details and diagrams are available.'

'Of course. Forgive me. You wouldn't happen to know where I might—?'

'The last I saw' – Mercer leaned forward with a confiding wink – 'she was on her way to the bar. Drown her sorrows. Shame. A very pretty girl, too!'

Solo received directions to the bar from him and managed to detach himself and head for it. His thoughts were confused. The presence of THRUSH agents and Sarah O'Rourke's sudden speechlessness added up to dirty play somewhere. But if copies of the paper were being freely distributed—?

The bar was in a long, low-ceilinged and dimly-lit room, not too crowded. She sat at a table in the far corner, all alone. As he neared her he saw that the picture he had seen at U.N.C.L.E. headquarters had understated her beauty, if anything, and contrary to Mercer's suspicions she didn't look at all affected by her drink, merely miserable – not drowning her sorrows but just dwelling on them.

'Mind if I join you?' he asked, gazing down at the delightful picture she made. Her figure was good enough to match her face, but as she looked up at him the effect of her beauty was marred just a little by the storm in her eyes.

'Yes I do mind!' she retorted, in a croaking whisper. 'I don't want to talk about anything, least of all that!' And she glared at the stapled sheets in his hand.

He put on his best smile, ignored her wrath, and sat down. 'There are several lines I could try at this point,' he murmured. 'I could make a remark about having a woman at a disadvantage – speechless, you know? Or I could whip up a passionate interest in this stuff.' He frowned at the paper, then tore it neatly across. 'I could say, with absolute honesty, that you're the prettiest girl I've laid eyes on in a very long while and that I'm just trying to figure out some way of getting to know you. Or' – and he shrugged – 'I could tell you the plain cold truth. You're a scientist. Which would you rather have?'

Curiosity battled against irritation in her and won. 'What

6

do you mean, the cold plain truth?' She massaged her throat. 'About what?'

'About why you should so suddenly and conveniently lose your voice just before you were going to deliver a paper on an obscure topic. No, let me talk a bit. Your paper deals with some discovery made by Dr. Michael O'Rourke, and somebody didn't want you to give it, so they slipped you something to paralyse your vocal chords. The question is – why?'

To his surprise she suddenly turned a glorious smile on him, enough to make him tingle all over. 'You're having me on,' she whispered. 'I was carefully warned that you Americans are the crafty ones, with every trick in the book up your sleeves, but I never expected anything so wild as that!'

'You don't believe me?'

'I do!' she protested. 'I remember now – he was a long skinny Chinaman with a cigarette-holder and gilded finger-nails. Very sinister.' And she used her glorious smile again to elevate his blood pressure. 'Thank you, Dr. Solo. You've managed to take my mind off my disappointment, and I'm very grateful to you for that, anyway.'

'All right,' he said, deciding to follow up his advantage swiftly, 'let me do one more little thing for you. I know quite a bit about the kind of drug one uses for this kind of thing.' That much was true enough. 'It will be purely temporary in its effect. I can show you how to hasten your recovery from it.'

'You can? And how would that be?'

'Just sit still one moment; I'll be right back.' He rose and went to the bar, to return promptly carrying a half-bottle of Smirnoff. Her blue eyes travelled from the vodka to his face and registered distaste.

'Ah, now you've spoiled it. Trying to get me drunk – that's the oldest dodge in the world!'

'Not so fast!' he cautioned. 'You aren't going to *drink* this. Now, do we go to my room, or yours?' He put on his most frank smile, and noted her bewilderment. She reacted just as he had hoped she would and rose to her feet.

7

'You're a trier, I'll say that for you. And I'll feel a lot safer in my own room.' He bowed gravely and she took his arm like a princess. More than one pair of envious male eyes followed them as they left the bar. There was mild apprehension in her expression as she led him to her room and waited for him to close the door.

'And now what?' she demanded, in that husky scrap of voice that was becoming very attractive to his ears.

'Bathroom,' he said, leading the way, 'and a large glass.' He poured, saving just a couple of fingers in the bottle, then handed her the glass with the command, 'Gargle! Be sure you spit it out, now, or my reputation will be mud!'

'*Your* reputation! I should be ashamed of myself for not thinking of it sooner. I *ought* to know about alcohol, seeing that I work with the stuff.'

'Good! All right, I'll leave you alone now. I'd rather not stand by and watch good liquor going to waste, even if it is in a good cause. The thing about vodka is that it won't make you smell like a distillery afterwards.'

She held the glass and looked at him with a lovely frown. 'I think I owe you some kind of apology, don't I?'

'Forget it. I'm always being misunderstood. What I *would* like from you, though, is a chance to look at your *original* paper.'

She noticed the stress on the word 'original', and frowned again. 'I don't see why. There's a hundred copies downstairs. Still, help yourself. It's in my briefcase, in there on the dresser.'

He heard her gargling as he found the case and zipped it open. This really was the original, judging by the typing, and the creases and fingermarks on the paper. He scowled at it, wishing he had the necessary expertise to understand the finer points. Casting a calculating eye over the available light, he got out his tiny cigarette-lighter camera and was all set to photograph the sheets when she called from the bathroom, still husky but much louder:

'You can *have* the paper, and welcome. I'm not likely to be wanting it any more now.'

'Thank you very much.' He folded the sheet slowly, slid

8

it into an inside pocket and strolled back to where she was still gargling. 'Are you taking part in anything else in this distinguished gathering?'

'No. I came only to deliver that talk and to hear some of the others. I'll be catching a plane home in the morning.'

'Back to Cooraclare Castle,' he murmured, and she choked in the middle of a gargle, coughed, regained her breath and stared at him.

'You seem to know a lot about me!'

'And I'd like to know a lot more,' he said, smiling. 'Look, there's a farewell dance this evening, the usual thing. Why don't I meet you there, and then you'll be able to tell me all sorts of fascinating things about molecules and yeast and things? Would you?'

She hesitated a moment, then gave him that high-voltage smile of hers again. 'I'd love to, just so long as I can count on getting a dance or two into the bargain. Are you sure it's the yeast you're interested in?'

'That' – he smiled – 'and other things.' He put the bottle down on the edge of the washbasin. 'Here – keep this for one more treatment later on. See you tonight – in full voice, I hope!'

Back in his own room he unclipped the pencil transceiver from his breast pocket and spoke sombrely into it: 'Open channel D.' As Waverly's voice came through he outlined the situation briefly. 'If she was doped to stop her talking, and I think she was, then it's possible the pertinent information is in her head and not on paper,' he concluded. 'Something that would have emerged in the questions afterwards. However, I have her own copies of the lecture notes and I'll send them over by messenger at once. Perhaps our experts can gather a clue or two from them.'

'With two hundred specialists right there on the spot I doubt if there is anything they've missed that we can find,' Waverly said dryly.

'The clues,' Solo explained, 'are for *me* to go on. I'm meeting her at the dance this evening. She should be in voice by then, and it will be my last chance – she's booked to fly home tomorrow. I can get her to talk, but how am I

9

supposed to carry on an intelligent conversation unless I have some notion what she's talking about?'

'Very well, Mr. Solo; get the papers to us and I'll see what the laboratory can do in the way of a synopsis for you. In the meantime you'll just have to use your imagination.'

'One more matter, sir.' Solo sighed. 'It could be that THRUSH won't *want* Miss O'Rourke to fly out in the morning. If they've tried to silence her once already they may do it the hard way next time.'

'Quite so. You'll have to watch out for that, Mr. Solo, won't you?' Waverly switched off.

Solo returned his transceiver to his pocket, shaking his head grimly. The majority of commanders fall into the sin of being unable to delegate authority for actions and insist on supervising everything personally. Waverly would never do that, but Solo couldn't help thinking he tended to go a bit too far in the opposite direction and assume that his men would somehow be successful at anything he told them to do. It was a very great compliment, of course, but Solo sighed as he contemplated just what was involved this time. He had to keep Sarah O'Rourke's good will to the point where she would babble to him whatever secrets there might be about synthetic yeast – and then he had to try to understand whatever it was she told him. Meanwhile he had to make sure that THRUSH didn't come up with any more dirty tricks against her – or himself, for that matter.

And in between times, have fun! he thought wryly, and decided to take a shave and shower and freshen up generally. It was futile to try and guess just what it was THRUSH was after, so he didn't bother, but he did find it hard to believe that anyone so utterly fresh and wholesome as Sarah O'Rourke could be involved in the kind of evil THRUSH would seek.

He was still pondering that thought as he went to pick her up for the dance, but he forgot it as soon as he saw her. This time her dress was two shades darker than her eyes, and it revealed the interesting fact that she was

10

roses-and-cream complexion all over. Almost all over, anyway. He stared in appreciation, and she went pink and timid.

'Is it all right?' she whispered. 'I bought it on purpose, as soon as I got here. I would never have the nerve to wear anything as bold as this back home. Nor the opportunity either.'

'Ireland's loss is my gain,' he said gallantly, 'and it is very much all right.' He extended his arm to lead her to the elevator. 'I had no idea biochemistry was such an interesting subject.'

She nodded gently as if confirming something to herself, and it wasn't until they were actually on the dance floor that he remembered he was supposed to *be* a biochemist. In chagrin at his slip he searched urgently for some safe topic of conversation while they danced.

'I had expected a crowd,' he said. 'The attendance figure was given as two hundred but there can't be a quarter of that number here.'

'All sorts of reasons for that. These are professional people, with not much time to spare, and not very good at frivolity anyway. A lot of them will be on their way home by this time. Just what are you, Mr. Solo?'

'Why do you ask?'

'Because I checked up on you in the professional register, and you're not there at all!'

'That does it, then – I'm unmasked. I'm a spy, snooping around to find out all your professional secrets.'

She laughed, and he found it a delightful sound. 'You'd be wasting your time with me, then,' she said. 'I've no secrets to hide at all. Uncle is the one with all the secrets.'

'Uncle?' Solo echoed, startled, then caught himself and grinned. 'Oh, you mean your Uncle Michael?'

'Who else? If it wasn't for him I wouldn't be here. He's the genius with all the secrets. I'm just a voice. And not even that, this afternoon.'

'Don't worry about it,' he said, as he whirled her across the floor. 'The voice is fine now.' She moved delightfully,

11

and as he held her close there was just the suspicion of perfume about her. Just right. If only he didn't have to concentrate on other, less agreeable, matters.

'Suppose I were a scientist, a biochemist,' he murmured, 'and suppose you've just read your learned paper. I'm in the audience. I want to ask a hot question. What might it be?'

She frowned prettily as they revolved in time to the music. 'That's a terrible question. It might be anything. Actually, my paper is only a description of two new and unusual molecules, with a general idea of the way to make them and some hints as to what their properties might be. If you wanted to know more about those, I couldn't tell you. My uncle does that part, him and Bridget. I'm in the molecular engineering department – the way to make them. And I'd not be free to tell too much about that, either, you see, because it's the details of the process of manufacture that is the real secret. That's what we're trying to sell. And I don't know it all anyway, only bits.'

Solo, trying to fit this into what he knew of the situation, caught sight of an elderly man, stout and red-faced, who was obviously struggling to attract his attention from the edge of the floor. Or someone's. His – or Sarah's?

'I think,' he murmured, 'that you have a fan. Someone trying to catch your eye. Over there, see?'

'I recognize him, from pictures,' she said. 'That will be Professor Amazov. He's one of the very few here who would really be in a position to understand and appreciate Uncle's discoveries.'

'One of the few? But aren't they all biochemists?'

She chuckled, the delicious sound tickling all his nerves at once. 'You are the darling innocent, aren't you now? Trying to pass yourself off as a real scientist. As anyone could tell you, biochemistry is a hodgepodge of specializations of all kinds – chemistry at one end, biology at the other, and all sorts in between: cytologists, serologists, immunologists, chemical engineers, specialists in X-rays and crystallography, virology, genetics, photosynthesis, energy-transfer systems—'

12

'Point taken,' he interrupted. 'Perhaps you'd better talk to the real expert while I just listen and take notes?'

'I'd much rather just go on dancing with you,' she declared, with such obvious sincerity that he was shaken for a moment. Such transparent honesty was rare in his experience. Regretfully he steered her in the general direction of a corner table. Then he tensed suddenly, as his roving gaze caught and held the cold stare of one of the THRUSH men he had seen and recognized earlier. Dancing on, he saw the other, and a chill ran along his spine. So they weren't through yet! And they had him spotted, too. He made a fast decision, spun her to a chair and sat her down. He saw Amazov puffing and thrusting through the thin crowd, until he was almost at hand.

'I must go,' he said to Sarah. 'Just for a moment. Very urgent. I'll be right back.' He turned to bow to the professor, who dismissed him with a snort and spun on Miss O'Rourke abruptly.

'Young woman, I've been wanting to speak to you ever since I saw that ridiculous nonsense you've issued as a paper. It was utter rubbish—'

Solo slipped away smoothly, carrying with him a vivid memory of Sarah's beautiful bewilderment. Quick steps got him through a door into a quiet room. He took out his pencil-speaker hastily, asked for the channel, and got Waverly's reply.

'Anything on that paper yet? I'm in over my head here.'

'I was about to call you, Mr. Solo. The laboratory reports that the paper is some kind of joke or hoax – they say it's meaningless, particularly the molecular diagrams.'

Solo pulled down his eyebrows in a frown. 'There's a Professor Amazov busy telling my fair lady that very same thing right now. Do you detect a smell, sir?'

'I do. I suspect Miss O'Rourke managed to lose her speaking voice at a very convenient moment.'

'A fraud, you mean? Why would she do that? There are only a few people here who would know any different. No, wait—' Solo caught his breath. 'You mean she's trying to sell a phoney to THRUSH? And they silenced her to stop

13

her advertising it too much? Because if that's the case, then Amazov is in the process of tearing it up, and she's in bad trouble.'

He shut off, hesitating a moment in a struggle between two alternatives. Believing anything menacing was over, he had left his gun in his room. Now he itched to go and get it, fast. But it was even more urgent to get back to her before Amazov spilled all the beans. He made his decision, whirled and headed for the dance-floor. The music had struck a momentary pause as he entered and headed for the corner. He could see the professor, red-faced and dogmatic, laying down a stricture with hard gestures, and Sarah staring angrily back at him.

And then, from behind him and just to the right, he heard the very familiar *cough-plop* sound of a silenced pistol. He saw Amazov stiffen, straighten up, and then slump limply face down on the table. Sarah backed off and screamed, a big, full-throated, full-bodied scream that killed the hubbub in the room absolutely dead.

Solo hurried forward. For ten seconds he was the only person who was moving in the room. Reaching the table, he put out a hand to steady her and she clung to him like a child. He glanced at the ring of white faces around them, then at the slumped body.

'Get the police,' he said, crisp and cold. 'And a doctor!'

The doctors were there first, for this room was full of them, of various kinds. Solo had time to learn that scientists are just as hysterically nervous as are lay people when confronted with something outside their own field. He held Sarah tight, and insisted that nobody touched anything until the law arrived. Nobody was to move, nobody to leave, he added. Standard routine, because there was nothing else to do at this moment. And in the waiting he cudgelled his brain to fit this last item – of murder – into an already confused picture. Why shoot Amazov? It didn't make any kind of sense at all!

Then came the minions of the law, very prompt and efficient, and all his precariously-held picture began to fall apart into a nightmare. The lieutenant was brisk and com-

14

petent, his men alert. It took only minutes to verify what had actually happened, where everybody had been sitting and standing when the shot had been fired. From where had the sound come? What had it sounded like?

Sarah managed to give her testimony with reasonable accuracy. Half-a-dozen onlookers backed her up. All the pieces fitted. Shot in the back. From *that* direction. Who had been in *that* direction at that time? Solo grimaced as one witness after another declared that *he* had been 'right there' when the shot had sounded. And he had been the only one in the room who hadn't seemed stunned into immobility by the killing. Even Sarah had to admit that.

'I'm not armed,' Solo protested, more irritated than anything by the ironic twist of events.

The lieutenant ignored him. 'Now where,' he mused aloud, 'would you be most likely to ditch the gun?' He wondered, and looked, and pointed, and one of his cohorts went and looked, and found a gun clumsily hidden in a potted-palm. He picked it up and carried it strictly according to the rule-book, a pencil inserted in the barrel. Solo shook his head sadly as he saw it.

'Let me save you the trouble,' he said. 'It's mine.' There was no room for doubt. The gun, which looked something like a Luger but wasn't, bore his initial, an 'S' engraved on the butt. And it was unique in other ways, as the lieutenant's expression showed when he inspected it. He was still staring at it as the police surgeon straightened up from his quick inspection of the body.

'Damnedest gunshot wound I ever saw, lieutenant,' he declared. 'The man's alive. Very little hemorrhage. But he's completely out cold. Anesthetized!'

'My gun,' Solo repeated wryly. 'May I show you?' He reached out and took the weapon from the lieutenant's hand, and four police positives appeared like conjuring tricks, all looking right at him. He smiled thinly, broke the magazine, and showed one of the cartridges with its needle-pointed capsule. Leading all the intent eyes in that direction, he managed to slip another one unseen into his pocket. He composed his features into a tight smile.

'Sorry about this,' he said to Sarah, who looked stunned. 'It's all a mistake, of course. I'll explain, sometime later.' Then he offered his wrists to the law and shrugged. 'Shall we go, gentlemen?'

The cell was clean and not too uncomfortable, all things considered. As soon as he was alone, Solo drew out his transceiver and put out the call.

'Open channel D.' As Waverly came on he steeled himself to recite the details in cold words, sparing himself not at all. Only at the end did he give way to a personal comment. 'It must have been manna from heaven for THRUSH,' he growled. 'They were dying to find some way to silence Amazov, and I was the goat. The fact's obvious, now that it's too late.'

'It isn't obvious to me, Mr. Solo, not yet. Why should they want to silence Amazov?'

'Because he was about the only person there who knew enough to understand the finer points of her paper. The way I see it, in its original form it gave away a little too much information. THRUSH didn't want that, so they got at it, altered it enough to make it meaningless, let her go ahead and run off a stack of copies, then doctored her drink so that she lost her voice, thereby making sure she wouldn't read it through herself. Doesn't it make sense? Otherwise there was no reason for her to read her own paper. Once she lost her voice, and her scheduled lecture time, she just didn't bother any more, naturally.'

'That's a very ingenious theory, Mr. Solo.'

'Isn't it? And it's the only thing that fits. There's obviously something pretty potent about those molecules as originally described. I suggest the laboratory make some more tests on that script, this time looking for erasures and alterations. They might even be able to restore the original version.'

'Yes. We'll do that. Good thinking, Mr. Solo, if a trifle tardy. Now, I suppose, I shall have to pull strings to get you out of there!'

'Yes, sir.'

'I don't like it. I shall have to ask favours. I remind you that we are supposed to come to the assistance of the duly constituted authorities, not to ask them to help *us*!'

'No, sir.'

'Very well. I think I can manage to "spring" you, if that's the word, in time to have you catch Miss O'Rourke's flight.'

'To Ireland?'

'It seems to be indicated.'

'You think THRUSH is going to let her get away?'

'Not "get away", Mr. Solo. To return home. If your thinking is accurate it will be to THRUSH's interest to see her safely onto that plane and off home without suspecting anything. They will of course try to stop you from going with her, or from learning anything from her. That's why you're in jail at the moment.'

Solo put away his instrument and spent a bitter moment in deep thought. It was nice to think that he would be seeing more of Sarah, but that said, the rest was sour to his taste. A night in the cells! What a comedown for U.N.C.L.E.'s top field agent! He could vividly imagine the insufferable grins and smirks from his colleagues when the information leaked out, as it certainly would once he was turned loose. He could almost hear the uniformed men passing the word, the plain-clothes squads spreading the tasty tidbit of scuttle-but.

'Yeah, sure! One of those fancy U.N.C.L.E. agents tripped right over his big flat feet, and we had to pick him up, dust him off and send him back home to Uncle, safe and sound!'

He writhed at the acid thought, rejecting it as insufferable. In sudden determination he cast an appraising eye around the bleak cell. It shouldn't be so hard to escape, at that. He was debating ways and means, not wanting to do too much damage to the taxpayers' property, when he heard the stolid approach of feet and saw the uniformed figure of his host for the night. He was a burly and overly jovial man, his crooked grin showing that he had already heard something of the inside story.

'Sort of a change for us to have distinguished company

17

here,' he said. 'Sorry the imperial suite isn't available right now.'

Solo smiled equably. 'It's not worth the trouble. I'm not staying.'

'That's right – I heard we're going to have to let you out.'

'With my property, I trust?'

'The trick gun, you mean? Oh sure. I have it right here.' The officer produced it, passed it butt-first through the bars. 'Kinda cute, but personally I prefer the Magnum. You hit a man, he stays hit, know what I mean? A man's gun.'

Solo hefted the weapon, smiled again. 'Empty, naturally.'

'Just one of those things,' the officer apologized. 'Routine. You know? Wouldn't want you to get ambitious or anything. No hard feelings, naturally. Like a cup of coffee?'

'That's a kind thought. Thank you.' He watched the solicitous policeman tread away whistling, felt for the spare cartridge he had managed to sneak, and held it in his fingers thoughtfully. Load up? Hardly. He wouldn't want to shoot the man without extreme provocation, and you can't properly threaten someone with a gun that he believes to be empty. On an impulse he hurriedly unscrewed the capsule end and secreted it between two fingers, then moved to s on his bunk. The jailer came back with a jug and two paper cups, dragged out a key-ring and unlocked the door, pushing it open.

'I'll join you,' he suggested amiably. 'Easier than passing the things through the bars; and you're not going to try any rough stuff, are you?'

Solo grinned and moved to the far end of the bunk to give himself safe room. 'I'd be a fool to try rough tactics with you,' he murmured. 'You'd probably tear my arm off and beat my head in with it and never turn a hair. What do we talk about?'

'Tricks of the trade,' the officer suggested, pouring a cup and passing it with a long arm. 'I bet you know a few, hey?'

'Some!' Solo nodded. 'Of course we're pretty helpless

without the technology. The trick gadgets. You know? A gun without slugs isn't much use, is it? But there are other ways.' He held the cup delicately, watching the other man pour his own. 'For instance, there's this. I could make a jerk, a gesture of some kind, a gasp – and point – and say, "Hey! Look there!" ' – 'The man's head moved instinctively, and Solo darted his empty hand at the cup, snatching it away as the officer swung swiftly back again. 'And that would give me just enough time to slip something into your drink. Not that I'd really do it, of course; that was just an instance.'

'Yeah!' The jailer eyed his cup dubiously. 'Just an instance. You wouldn't try anything funny on me, would you?' Solo pretended to sip at his cup, watching intently, seeing the doubt grow and spread and become certainty. 'Just a minute there. Maybe you *wouldn't* try to slug me with dope, but I'm not so sure! Here, you drink it! I'll have *that* one!'

Solo frowned protestingly. 'Oh, come on, you don't really believe I'd—?'

'You have mine!' the officer insisted, suddenly harsh. 'And I'll take yours. Come on!'

Solo shrugged ruefully and accepted the exchange, carefully holding the new cup away from his mouth. The jailer glowered, took a healthy sip from his cup and swallowed, savouring the taste, his eyes hard on Solo.

'This is good coffee, mister. Go ahead a⸱ ⸱d drink. I want to see you. Go on!' He finished his own cup, cru⸱⸱⸱pled it in his hand and leaned belligerently forward. 'What's ⸱a ⸱⸱ ⸱t-ter? Lost your thirst? Cute trick's backfired on you again?' He glared at Solo, waiting.

Ten seconds later the answer didn't interest him at all. Solo was just in time to catch him from rolling off the bunk onto the floor of the cell. He snored peacefully as he lost his uniform tunic.

'Comes of having a nasty suspicious mind,' Solo murmured. 'You're a bit too old to learn new tricks, friend.'

Ten minutes later, having plodded placidly past the desk-sergeant in his borrowed clothes – at this hour no one was

19

paying very much attention anyway – he discarded the tunic in a conveniently dark doorway and went on his way.

Twenty minutes later Miss Sarah O'Rourke awoke from an exciting dream to the more exciting but frighteningly realistic sensation of a firm hand over her mouth.

A familiar voice murmured, 'This is another way of rendering someone speechless. Shall we agree not to scream for a bit?' She gathered her wits, nodded, and the hand went away. In the gloom she recognized Napoleon Solo sitting on the edge of her bed.

'How did you get here?'

'Skip the trivia and listen. Have you gathered by now that someone wanted to stop Amazov from talking to you too long? All right; now what did he say?'

'Not very much, at all. He had it in his head that my molecular diagrams were all wrong. And that's silly, for didn't I draw them myself?'

'But somebody altered them before you had the copies run off. I've had your paper checked, and it *is* nonsense. That's for sure. So it follows that there is something very important about those diagrams. You're sure you don't know anything about the effects?'

'Nothing at all. What's all this about, anyway?'

'I don't know it all, only this – that you have some dangerous knowledge tucked away in that pretty head of yours, and certain parties are keen to see that it doesn't leak out. There's a chance they might try to silence you again, more permanently this time.'

'Are you deliberately trying to give me the cold shivers?'

'I am. And I hope I'm succeeding. The people I have in mind are good people to be scared of, believe me.' He sat back and eyed her thoughtfully. As she sat up in bed in a white linen nightdress, she looked very lovely – and extremely vulnerable. He got out his wallet, extracted a card, handed it to her, and she gave a giggle that was just short of hysteria.

'This is a crazy time to start being formal, isn't it?' she laughed.

20

'No formality about it. That card is bugged. See that you keep it safe and handy. If at any time between now and when you board your plane you are in any danger, or distress of any kind, you take that card and fold it, just once, down the middle.' He made a gesture in demonstration. 'That will trigger a signal that I will be able to detect and follow. An alarm. All right?'

'Holy Mother!' She stared at the pasteboard in her fingers. 'I believe you mean it!' He stood up from the bed and smiled grimly.

'I do. Don't forget now. Keep it handy. See you on the plane tomorrow – I hope!'

'You're coming along too?'

'You bet. You don't think I'd let a gorgeous creature like you get away from me as easily as that, do you?'

The new day was just half an hour old as he entered *The Masked Club* on the ground floor of the old whitestone, and from there made his way into the headquarters which held the people of his arduous profession. A glance at the pin-lighted 'state' board told him Waverly was still awake and in business. He shook his head at it. That old man seemed able to get by with little or no sleep and could always be counted on to be handy when things were happening. Solo made his way swiftly to the lead-lined office that was Waverly's own, the only room in that steel-walled maze boasting a window. Perhaps, he thought, he could surprise the old man yet.

But Waverly merely looked up at him from beneath his shaggy grey eyebrows and murmured, 'I had expected you ten minutes ago. I suppose it *is* difficult to get a cab at this hour. I've been studying the latest reports on those papers. You were quite right – they *have* been tampered with.'

Solo sighed. 'And the original version?'

'Something quite new, according to our experts. They are running a set of computer simulations at this moment to try and estimate the possible effects. It will take time, and will be only a guess, at that. We won't know for sure until we've tried the stuff on a human volunteer.'

21

'Try me,' Solo said instantly. 'After all, I did make a bit of a hash—'

'Don't be silly, Mr. Solo. I can't afford to expend you as a guinea-pig. You're much too valuable to be wasted in that manner. In any case, you have problems of your own, if you're to catch that flight tomorrow.'

Solo shrugged and went away thoughtfully. As he busied himself with the minor things, such as loading up his pistol and setting up an electronic ear that would listen out for a cry for help from Sarah, he mused about this other, less spectacular side of U.N.C.L.E., which held the nameless and unsung toilers who took the calculated and cold-blooded chances in the obscurity of the back room. That was one aspect he didn't care to think about too often. Soon somebody would try a measured dose of Uncle Mike's new synthetic molecule, and would sit and wait while others watched him with clinical detachment. All would wonder and be on the alert to observe and study whatever new hell-ishness was due to be let loose on a long-suffering world. And, if that unnamed hero were very lucky, he would sur-vive to write up his notes. And this was in the day's work.

The exercise had its point. Reflections like this were what a field agent needed to inspire him to try his damnedest not to waste that sacrifice. Solo applied his mind to devising some way of getting himself on the plane to Ireland all in one piece. 'They' would want Sarah safely back home. 'They' would believe Napoleon Solo still safely in jail, and the police would not be in a hurry to advertise otherwise. With those two cards, plus an aesthetic liking for simplicity, he had his plans made before he drifted off to sleep.

His sleep was brief. He was up and away from U.N.C.L.E. headquarters long before anyone would have expected, long before certain observers took up their posts. They were intended to see a man leaving with a small case, a man who neither advertised his presence nor did anything to conceal it; and this they saw. Even the uninformed ob-server would have guessed, by his appearance, that here was someone of reasonable importance departing on a mis-

22

sion of some worthy nature. The agent was one Jerry Willmott, and his ability to look like a dignified minor official was not the least of his many attributes. Keen eyes monitored his sedate procession by taxi from U.N.C.L.E. headquarters to Kennedy International Airport. Brisk instructions were given, purposeful men began to close in on him, and the line-up for the Customs check became slightly agitated.

Miss Sarah O'Rourke, in good time and safely through, spent anxious moments scanning the shifting crowd in the hope of seeing a familiar face, until her attention, like everyone else's, was drawn to the scuffle at the counter. Willmott protested, sternly and with dignity. Several men, he claimed, had jostled him. One had knocked his case from his hand to the ground, whereupon it had mysteriously burst open. The officials, suspicious of him, listened with patent disbelief to his story. They inspected the baggage, and then his person, carefully. They heard his disclaimer that those wrist-watches, and that whisky – actually in his pocket – were his own. Planted, of course, he said. They'd heard it all many times before. They invited him inside. But then Willmott changed his tune to a slightly different key.

'You'll notice,' he pointed out silkily, 'that I'm wearing gloves. Now can we have a fingerprint check on all those articles you've discovered and that I'm supposed to be trying to smuggle? – and then compare the prints with those of certain parties I can point out from here?'

Sarah watched the impending scuffle as various people tried to leave, with the airport police trying just as urgently to stop them, and sighed to herself. New York, she thought, was far too exciting a place to stay in for very long. She was glad to be going home. But she felt disappointed, all the same, for that nice Mr. Solo had said— And then she started as a deferential voice intruded on her distressful thoughts.

'We should be getting along to the plane, Miss. It will go soon. It will not wait for the crooked ones. Permit me to carry your bag, yes?'

The speaker was slim, not too tall, obviously trying to

23

be friendly. By the sound of his clipped English, and to judge by his brief black moustache, neatly pointed beard and brilliant smile, he was Italian. Although shielded by darkened glasses, his eyes seemed honest enough. 'You're very kind,' she said. 'I had hoped to meet somebody, but I suppose you're right; they won't keep the plane waiting, will they?'

It wasn't until her strange companion had gallantly escorted her all the way to her seat and stowed her personal baggage in the rack over her head that she realized she didn't know his name. In response to her question he smiled his brilliant smile, sat himself in the seat by her side and said:

'Not yet. Not while we are still on the ground, eh? Once we are on the way, it will be different.'

They didn't have long to wait. Doors slammed, the engines picked up power, and there came the familiar warning. 'Fasten your seat-belts, please!' Sarah gave up her last lingering hope that Napoleon Solo would somehow make a dramatic last-minute appearance, and determined to forget all about him. She turned in time to see her companion in the act of peeling off his pointed beard, sighing with every evidence of relief.

'You didn't really think I'd let you get away, did you?' he chuckled.

'Mr. Solo! But why—?'

'The opposition were on the look-out for somebody. So we put somebody there for them to see, and deal with – while I slipped by in the confusion.'

'That poor man at the Customs!'

'Jerry will know exactly what to do. Right now, three or four THRUSH agents are having to explain how their fingerprints come to be all over the contraband he was supposed to be carrying. Do them all the good in the world.' Solo took a moment to glance round the seated passengers, and his smile was a shade harder as he brought it back to her. 'Let us not start counting any premature chickens, however. They were smart enough to plant two more on this flight. Easy now; they won't start anything while we're in

24

the air. They want you home safe and sound. It's me they'll try to get playful with, and they won't try that until we're at the other end.'

'You're trying to scare me again!' she accused, wide-eyed.

'Not for the world.' Solo smiled reassuringly. 'I only want you to know it's *my* neck they're after, not yours. Isn't that comforting to know?'

Sarah frowned dubiously.

CHAPTER TWO

'THE SPIRITS OF ME ANCESTORS ARE WATCHING YE'

ILLYA NICKOVETCH KURYAKIN lay stretched out, soaking in the sunshine, on the heather-padded slope of a hillside; tinted glasses were over his pale blue eyes and his straw-yellow thatch of hair was hidden under a soft hat that was tilted to shade his face. He was untidy but comfortable in a faded check-shirt and battered old slacks. He looked half asleep.

Close by his right elbow a stout staff stood erect, its lower end rammed firmly into the turf, a battered old tweed jacket apparently casually slung over its top to afford a measure of shade. The jacket adequately concealed a metal dish, at the focus of which hung a tiny but highly sensitive microphone. A thin wire crawled down the staff and fed into the canvas pack that was currently doing duty as a pillow. Within that pack the wire led into an amplifier. Another wire from the amplifier lay along the heather and stretched to Kuryakin's right ear, and to the tiny speaker hidden there. From time to time he might have been seen to reach out and touch the staff, to twist it minutely, just a fraction, in order to keep that snooping microphone accurately aimed at two people down below.

They were almost a mile away and were going through the motions of playing a round of golf over the Conway Club greens. They had the course to themselves, and thought they were secure from observation. Yet Kuryakin could hear virtually every word they said, and found it most interesting.

In his brief term on the job he had accomplished much. U.N.C.L.E.'s man in Limerick had briefed him up to date. He had lodgings in Ennis to match his walking-tour guise. He had seen and identified Trilli and his two henchmen, Schichi and Foden, and had estimated them all accurately. Trilli might look like an inoffensive rabbit, but he had the real brain and was as deadly as a snake. Schichi was big, burly, a typical Italian thug, handy with any kind of weapon but short on brains. Foden, now, was blond, Nordic, and smart. Also tough – he'd bear watching. He drove the hired Daimler that had brought Trilli to this unusual golf-match. He and Schichi had been left to wait in the clubhouse while Trilli and his companion played.

It made sense, Kuryakin mused, awarding Trilli credit for using his head. If you want to meet and talk with someone in secret, avoid the dark corners, the deserted houses, the secret room or the concealing hedge. There you are just asking somebody to sneak up and listen in. Your best bet is to pick a place right out in the open, without cover, where you can see possible interference coming miles away, and be warned.

Trilli had chosen well. It wasn't his fault that science had worked out a method of selecting sound vibrations over a long distance with all the accuracy of a telescope.

Kuryakin continued to listen. What made this conversation particularly interesting was the fact that Trilli was doing his dickering with a woman!

She was too far away for Kuryakin to observe her in detail. She wore a trim green cashmere sweater and short tweed skirt and he knew that she was Bridget O'Rourke. He also knew that she had a very pleasant voice, and by the skilful way she employed it that she was a very dangerous person indeed.

'I'm not blaming you for being careful,' she said. 'If you want to insist that you're just a representative of some big

26

chemical combine in Europe – which you refuse to name – then that's it, and good luck to it. But if you stick with that story, then you're stuck, you see? Because I'm telling you, straight out, that Uncle Mike positively will not deal with anything less than THRUSH itself. That's what he's after, and that's what he's going to have. You see?'

This was the third time she had invited Trilli to confess his true colours, and Kuryakin grinned at the Italian's reluctance to commit himself until he had something definite to go on.

'My dear young lady, always this talk about THRUSH!' he protested. 'I would prefer not to speak thus. First I wish to meet Dr. O'Rourke and discuss his new process. First I must know if it is any good. Then I talk business. But I do not buy a pig in a bag, you understand? This is not so unreasonable as all this wild talk about THRUSH. I never heard of that name before.'

'Ah now, I'll believe that when I see it snowing straight up!'

Her voice dwindled and Kuryakin squinted down at them, to see that they were now going through the motions of teeing up for the next hole. The Conway Club course lay like three sides of a box around the hill. The first nine holes took you three quarters of the way around, and the last nine brought you back again. It was a design that suited him very well, and if there were a small germ of curiosity in his mind as to why the greens had not been laid out to go completely around the hill, he refused to let it bother him.

He reached out to adjust the staff fractionally, and caught fragments of talk, mostly hers, concerning Uncle Mike. He had apparently been a hell-raiser in his young days, had heard bits and pieces about THRUSH, and had put them together to make a shrewd guess at the whole. He had told his niece his suspicions, and now she was repeating them to Trilli.

Listening, Kuryakin had to admit that she had most of her facts right. He was intrigued by the incongruity of it. Here against the green tranquillity of this quiet flower-strewn landscape, with its pastoral beauty and purple distances.

27

she spoke of a sinister world-wide organization, a nation without a home, a band of ruthless people whose only loyalty was to the Ultimate Computer, whose aim was to master the world. Using any technique that would work, no matter how evil, THRUSH took over a city, a council, an industry, or some vital service, and used it as its pawn. She knew all these facts, and related them in cheerful detail, as if thoroughly approving the work. She even knew about the Supreme Council of THRUSH. She went to some pains to make this point clear.

'I *know* Uncle Mike,' she declared. 'I know him better than anybody does. He won't sell his discovery, not to the big business you pretend to represent, not even to THRUSH, which you *do* represent!'

Trilli snorted. 'It is become ridiculous. You insist I am THRUSH, and then you say not even to THRUSH will he sell! What, then, does Dr. O'Rourke want?'

'He will contribute his genius in return for a full membership on the Supreme Council,' she said with flat conviction. 'You'll remember, he's King Mike in these parts, and h᷾ ᷼not one to give up power easily.'

Kᷤ ᷷yakin chuckled to himself. Trilli was in a spot now. Althouᵍʰ he had status within THRUSH he was very far from being *that* important. He was just a hireling, a field man and could make no rash promises. The Italian recovered his voice with an effort.

'You really think I am in a position to offer this?'

'Not you!' She was cheerful. 'But you can take the message back. And you can now meet Uncle Mike, seeing you've at last admitted you *are* THRUSH!'

Kuryakin lost his grin swiftly as he felt an urgent tingle from that sixth sense any agent must have if he is to survive long. Squinting urgently over his shoulder, he saw two men halfway up the right-hand slope of the hillside, one of whom was peering at him through binoculars.

One glance was enough to identify them as Schichi and Foden and to force him to make immediate decisions. There was no sense in standing his ground and hoping to play innocent with those two.

28

Kuryakin moved with deliberate speed. Rapid touches folded the dish and microphone into compactness and into the shoulder-pack. A wriggle got him into his jacket and the pack on his back.

A quick glance as he yanked the staff out of the turf showed his estimate to be accurate. Schichi and Foden were now moving towards him fast, hailing the two players at the same time, alerting them. A discreet withdrawal on his own part seemed best.

Kuryakin went up the hill swiftly, calculating the odds against him. If he could get over the crest, down the other side, and into the wilderness of bush and scrub, he could lose his pursuers easily. Of course they might shoot, but he didn't think they would, although there was an uncomfortable itch between his shoulder blades as he scrambled up the slope as fast as he could go.

He lost his footing for a gasping moment and tripped, going down on one knee by a wiry bush. In that same second the air where his head would have been was ripped by the violent passage of something that hurled on to smack into the grassy bank a yard ahead.

Kuryakin marked it, noting the absence of any sound of a shot. His left hand dug out the projectile as he rushed past and scrambled on up. His fingers told him what it was even before he managed to snatch a glance at it. They had used a golf ball. Judging by the way in which it had gouged into the ground, it had come from a powerful catapult or something similar. That would be Foden's idea. Ingenious fellow, Foden.

Kuryakin's habitually serious expression hardened as he appreciated the thinking. A man shot dead is an awkwardness, something to invite curiosity, but who would think it anything more than a sad accident if a man should be struck and killed with a golf ball, here right beside a golf course?

Panting, he tossed the ball away and went on. The hilltop was close now. From behind him he heard shouts. Halting at the crest, he weighed the prospect swiftly and shrugged off his pack. The way down was steep, but thick with heather. He dropped the pack between his feet, stood across it, gripped the straps, and gave a strangled groan as something hit him a hammer-blow in the small of his back.

Foden again, a damned good shot. Grinding his teeth against the kidney-ache, he squatted on his pack and shoved off, and down, tobogganing over the springy heather at a furiously jolting rate. It wasn't the smoothest ride in the world, but it was easily ten times as fast as anyone might follow on foot. Using his staff like an oar, and his heels desperately, he snatched a backward glance and saw all four of them appear on the crest above him.

He hit a bump and flew a short distance, landing with a bone-jarring jolt. Another snatched glance back. No sign of pursuit yet. He was going to make it.

The bottom came rapidly nearer. He steered valiantly, bouncing and bumping, seeking ahead for the best place to halt, trying to evade the bigger hummocks. He saw a shallow gully, and aimed for it. Beyond that was a very smooth and invitingly open green space. Thrusting savagely, he shot towards it, his knees up, his whole body braced for the jolt of stopping. There came one of those moments when time seems to stop and hold its breath. He saw the edge ahead, and knew that he was going to shoot out and drop like a ski-jumper, that the drop would be about ten or twelve feet onto that smooth green.

Then he realized there was something ominously suspicious about that smoothness, its greenness and softness. With one last breathless bump he was in mid-air and falling. And, with a supreme effort of will against his natural instinct to drop feet first and cushion his impact, he twisted and writhed, turned in mid-air and spreadeagled himself to fall flat on his back. Flat – with a great slap and splurge – into slimy green ooze!

A bog. Had he been wrong in his snap judgment, had it been turf, the shock would have broken his back. Instead, he was knocked breathless but otherwise unhurt. He lay still for a long moment. Some freak of acoustics brought him, faintly, the voices from up there.

Trilli snapped, 'If you are very quick, and go around, you will—'

'There's no need of that,' Bridget O'Rourke interrupted calmly. 'Whoever he is, he won't trouble us again. Never a one has come back up out of Kevin's Hole that I ever heard of!' There came a moment of mumbling and then her voice again, still cheery: 'Try it for yourself, and see. Slap one of your golf balls down on that green there, and see what happens to it!'

Seconds later there came a hiss, a smack, and the splatter of flying mud on his face as the ball impacted a yard from his head. Came more muttering, going away into the distance, and then silence. The ooze was up to his ears and in his hair. It felt cold and wet all along his back and legs. They were right to be confident. He felt himself sinking by gradual inches.

Panic screamed at the back of his mind, to be met and hurled back by his cold determination, his savage commonsense, his brain frantically surveying the enormous fund of out-of-the-way information he had gathered in the course of an arduous life. He separated fact from fantasy with urgent efficiency. Bog, marsh, quagmire, quicksand – none of these can actually 'suck' anything down, despite all legends, for the simple scientific reason that it is impossible to exert a downward suction on the free surface of any fluid. The entrapment action is simply that of a solid body resting on a fluidized bed exerting all its weight on a small area and thus displacing the less-solid support.

Had he landed feet-first, or had he tried to stand and struggle – as almost everyone does – he would have gone under in seconds. As he was now, with his weight dispersed over a large area, he was sinking very slowly. Yet he was still sinking.

The train of thought raced through his mind as he swivelled his eyes to study the situation without moving any more than he could help. The outlook was bleak. His ski-jump drop had deposited him virtually into the centre of the morass. In all directions but one he was some twelve to fourteen feet away from the first straggle of bushes which marked any firm footing. It is just possible to swim in mud, but progress is painfully slow and consumes enormous amounts of energy.

He surveyed the one spot that was closer, the edge over which he had slid. Horizontally it was no more than six feet away, but the surface was sheer smooth rock, standing straight up some eight or nine feet before it offered a ledge to grab at. The ooze crept to the corners of his mouth as he studied that rock-face. In his outflung right hand he still held his staff; the other hand gripped the straps of his pack. Then he knew he had no more time to waste in calculation.

Taking a good deep breath, he nerved himself, rolled over to his right towards the rock, swinging the pack over, slapping it into the mud, squirming his chest onto it, using its temporary buoyancy to gain him a thrust forward, his face clear of the stinking slime. Now he could almost have reached to touch the rock-face with his fingers, but he had sacrificed his reserve of buoyancy; he was wet all over and sinking fast. There was no time to waste. Up went his head and shoulders and down went the rest of his body, deep into the mire. With only seconds to spare he worked frantically at his staff, which was no ordinary shaft of wood, but a strong telescopic pole, highly useful as an extensible aerial, or a weapon, or, as now, to be stretched out and hooked onto a wall a fence – or a rocky ledge.

He freed and locked the hook with savage speed, slid out the extensions, hearing them click into place, the slime at his chin by now. Bearing down with his left arm, he strained up with the right, straight up, snagged the hook and pulled hard. Small stones and soil came away and rained down onto his face as the hook broke free. With the stinking slime now at his lip, numbing cold soaking his body, he made one more frantic lunge and catch, the glittering hook passing over the ledge.

And it held! He dragged on it, steady but hard, tensely, getting all his weight onto it by cautious degrees. Then he took hold with his other hand, got a savage grip – and heaved! The sweat sprang out on his face as the bog clung, reluctant to release its prey. He heaved again, shoulder-muscles tearing under the strain. And again, and now the slime fell back to his shoulders. With shivering care he walked his grip up the rod and heaved again, and again, until his waist, and then his hips, came free of the ooze.

His hands, arms and shoulders burned like fire. His missed a grip and hung for an agonized moment by one slipping hand until he could get it back again. The chill flame of determination drove him to fight one hand over the other and go on, and up, until there was stone under his fingers. Then an elbow. And then a space to get his knee on. And then he fell flat and breathless on his face in the heather and lay still.

In a while he was able to sit up. A while longer and he could stand. Then he wearily began to make his way down and around the death-trap green, through the wild country beyond, and eventually back to his lodgings. Most of the green sludge had dried and flaked away by then but he was still in a dreadful state, enough to make his landlady throw up her hands in dismay at the sight of him.

'Fell into a bit of bog, did you?' she cried, as he told her his own version of the truth. 'You're very fortunate to be alive to tell it. You'll be wanting a bath to get off the mud, and let me have those things of yours till I see whether I can get them cleaned up a bit for ye.' This suited him very well, for there are few places more private than a bathroom, and he had urgent need to discuss certain things with someone. Luxuriating in hot water and vapour, he put a call through to his Limerick contact.

'I'm going to need one or two things,' he said. 'It seems they want to play this the hard way.' And he winced as his muscles protested in the small of his back. That golf ball had *hurt!*

The Limerick office promised cooperation, and also had a little news for him: 'U.N.C.L.E. One has some first-run results on one of the O'Rourke molecules. Similar to serotonin, same type of thing, very probably a hallucinogen, but they're not sure about the full effects yet.'

'That's not surprising,' he returned. 'That kind of test could take weeks. I might get results faster by taking

33

a private look at the laboratory in the castle. I will want a run-down on the modifications Dr. O'Rourke has had installed, and an interior plan. Also—'

He specified his needs closely. He had had plenty of time to figure them out while trudging back from Kevin's Hole.

An ill-assorted foursome climbed out of Trilli's hired Daimler as Foden drew it to a halt within the forecourt of Cooraclare Castle. The three from THRUSH had little interest in its architecture or authenticity. They were more concerned with its potential as a fortress, noting that the walls were massive, the windows small and strong, and that there was a man up there by the crenellations watching their every move.

"'Tis only a small castle,' said Bridget airily, watching their eyes and accurately gauging their thoughts. 'Uncle Mike had it renovated and modernized, but it's just as strong as ever it was. I think we'll find him in the receiving room.'

She led them through a great arched doorway and into a vast stone-floored hall with a grand double staircase at the far end. A large man in dark livery stood at the top of those stairs, a shotgun held casually under his arm. The receiving room lay off the hall to the right and was noteworthy for being hung with many oil-paintings, every one of which bore a striking family resemblance to the sharp-eyed old man who sat now at the far end of a long table that filled most of the centre of the floor. He rose to his feet as they entered.

Michael O'Rourke had been a big and powerful man in his prime. He was gaunt now but still an imposing six foot three, with a gleam in his eye, his white hair and beard giving him something of the air of an Old Testament prophet.

'And who might it be who seeks the honour of approaching King Michael in the heart of his own little kingdom?' he demanded, with a smile that was no more than a showing of his white teeth.

'This is the one you've been waiting for, Uncle Mike.'

Bridget gestured to Trilli, who moved a hesitant step and stopped. 'He didn't want to admit it at all, but he's THRUSH all right. Dr. Vittorio Trilli, of Genoa. And that's Angelo Schichi – Karl Foden. Just friends.'

'I have not said I am THRUSH!' Trilli denied sharply.

The old man's smile grew into a leer. 'You've been in the district a week or two, mister. You've been asking a lot of interesting questions about meself, and O'Brien's Beers, and such like. You have a couple of bully boys with you for bodyguard.' Bridget moved steadily forward as he was talking, to pass the length of the table and stand by his side.

'Trilli, that's your name, and you're a chemist. A good one, too. At least, you were, until you were allegedly killed in a peculiar accident about four years ago. That's strange now, isn't it? But it fits the THRUSH pattern. When they want a man badly, they arrange for him to "die", and then they have him, you see, body and soul. You're in the crunch, Mr. Trilli. Either you are a THRUSH agent, or you're an impostor, take your pick!'

'You are very well informed,' Trilli muttered, no longer rabbity-looking. 'If this is some kind of trap – a clumsy one—' And there was an evil-looking pistol in his hand all at once. Simultaneously Foden and Schichi stepped away, and they held guns too. All three stared steadily at O'Rourke. The old man's caprine beard twitched, but his eyes were like spears and his smile satanic.

'The spirits of me ancestors are watching ye,' he said, very softly; and Trilli glanced away ... and stiffened. Six of the oil-paintings had slid aside. In the dark cavities revealed, three on each side, stood men, large and ruddy-faced and ready, each with a shotgun levelled at him and his friends. 'A scatter-gun makes an awful bad mess at this range,' the old man pointed out. 'Ye said I'm well-informed, and so I am. I remind ye, I'm king in these parts. I'm well-served. But I'm a fair man, and I'm satisfied that you are what I think you are. I'm ready to talk a bit of business with you, if you'll put away the toys and be easy.'

Trilli shifted his gaze slowly from one pair of barrels to

35

another, and then shrugged in defeat, slipping his pistol out of sight again.

'Very well, we don't play games any more. We talk business.'

'That's fine. Bridget me dear, will you bring the bottle and glasses? There'll be high tea in a while. I make you welcome, good people, so long as you remember that I've a lot more handy buckoes like these scattered about the place. At one word from me they'd tear ye limb from limb and serve ye up as Mulligan, so they would. 'Tis a grand thing to be an absolute monarch.'

O'Rourke seated himself again and waved Trilli and his henchmen forward to take seats on either side of him.

Bridget produced the bottle and glasses. The old man reached into his corduroy smoking-jacket to produce a visiting card for Trilli. 'A token of goodwill,' he smiled. 'There's not many that has King Michael's personal card, believe me.' Trilli scowled, put the thing away in his breast pocket. In the thick silence they heard a clock, close by, chime out the half-hour.

'Unless something's happened to her,' Bridget declared, 'Sarah should be home soon.'

'She will, she will. Sarah's a reliable girl.'

'Your other niece?' Trilli wondered. 'The one you sent to the convention in New York to talk? Wasn't that foolish, giving away freely what you are trying to sell to me for a great price?'

The old man shook his head pityingly. 'When I'm on the Supreme Council I'll try to remember never to give you a job calling for intelligence. Think, man! D'ye think anybody will pay attention to anything announced freely and in public? Of course they won't. That's why I did it. And what did I give away, at all? Only the information that I know how to manufacture a new synthetic! That's all. Not *how* to make it, but that *I* know how to do it. And I do!'

'But you have put your process on the market for bids!'

'So I have, at a price that will be out of sight for anything less than one of the major manufacturing houses. And d'ye think they're going to rush to buy? Think again. They won't buy until they have some direct idea what the stuff is good for, and they can't know that until they make some to try – and they can't do that without the process method. Which I have. So, if they give it any thought at all, they'll shrug it off and forget it. Who's interested in some chance discovery in a brewery, anyway?' O'Rourke chuckled. 'But it will serve to stop nosy people sniffing round me heels, so it will.'

Trilli frowned. He didn't like this one bit. The old man was beyond doubt insane. But he had no room for argument now. 'Very well,' he declared. 'Now you will tell me, and show me, just what is so wonderful about this new molecule that you think you can dictate to THRUSH.'

The old man shed his jocularity instantly, and there was an edge to his voice as he said, 'I can hold the world to ransom, Dr. Trilli, not just THRUSH, with what I've discovered. *The whole world!* And I will, if I have to! It would be a bit easier and quicker with THRUSH on my side, but if I must, I will do it alone – and you can t҉e҉l҉l҉ ҉t҉h҉a҉t҉ back to your superiors, with the compliments of King Michael of Clare in Eire!'

'It's the truth, every word,' Bridget said. 'As for us giving away secrets in New York, you three must have left a trail a mile wide for that man to be snooping on us, by Conway.' She turned to her uncle. 'A silly little man was skulking on the hillside watching us. We chased him into Kevin's Hole. Right in. He'll be no more trouble at all.'

'It is all very well!' Trilli objected angrily. 'This is fine big talk. But nothing yet about what this precious chemical of yours can do. I must have evidence, proof, not just words. As you say, I am a chemist, a scientist. What I see with my own eyes, that I believe. Not talk!'

A soft footfall in the doorway brought all their heads around. Another large man stood there in an attitude of respect.

'Begging your pardon, your majesty, but there's an airport car belting up the road, with Miss Sarah in it and a man with her. An American, by the look of it.'

'Hah!' O'Rourke struck the table with an exasperated

37

palm. 'Isn't it always the same? The one curse of my life is what many another man would call a blessing – that I have two of the prettiest girls in the whole country living here with me, forever attracting young men like bees at a honey-pot! But—' and a devilish gleam came into his sharp eyes – 'perhaps this time I can turn a nuisance into good use. Perhaps this young man can be made to serve a good purpose. Donovan, make them welcome and take care of the baggage. Bridget, me darling, down to the cellar with you and bring back a can of the special, with an opener, and a glass'

She ⎯ ⎯le a brilliant smile and hurried away. O'Rourke turned to ⎯ ⎯ ⎯ and his smile was full of glee. 'You said you wanted evide⎯ ⎯ some proof of what my synthetic can do to a man, didn't yo⎯ Well now, just be still, let me do the talking, and you shall se⎯ ⎯ yourself.'

By the time the car reached the forecourt of the castle, Napoleon Solo was properly impressed by the pile. It wasn't quite as big as he had imagined from the picture, but it looked respectably old and solid.

As he paid off the car, Sarah chattered away. 'I'm sure I don't know what Uncle Mike will say about me bringing you home with me like this. He's not much of a hand for company. He prefers to meet people professionally by appointment at the brewery, and not at all at home, not unless it's something extra special. In a way, I'm breaking all the rules, just for you. But after everything you've told me about those wicked people trying to steal his discovery and everything, I'm sure it is the best thing for you to tell him all about it yourself and see what he says about it.' She paused for a rare breath and resumed, 'I know he wouldn't believe a word of it if I just told him myself. I'm not sure that I believe it myself, even if that poor man was shot and everything, at the dancing last night, poor Professor Amazov—'

Solo sighed inwardly and let the flood ripple over him. If she had a flaw, he thought, it was this regrettable tendency to chatter steadily on at great length. That, plus an equally unfortunate inability to believe anything he told her, particularly about THRUSH. He hadn't tried very hard to convince her about the two THRUSH agents on the plane because he'd had his own designs on them, which had called for innocence, on the surface at any rate. A long time ago he had learned certain bits of useful information from a master locksmith on how to make ordinary locking devices behave in most un-ordinary ways. That information, long unused but never forgotten, had proven most useful at the end of their uneventful flight. He had not known for sure whether the two agents had intended anything malicious towards him; but taking that for granted, he had acted accordingly.

Seat-belts are curious anomalies. You fasten them for a brief while on take-off and then they remain utterly unused until landing is imminent, when you are required to fasten them again, for a brief while, until the plane is safely down. In between times, they just hang there. He had waited for the moment when those two particular seats had been deserted and had then applied just a little expert knowhow – and everyone else had filed calmly from the plane while the two unhappy THRUSH men had still been vainly trying to undo the catches on their belts. And so he and Sarah had passed uneventfully out of the airport and into the first available taxi. A neat and effective plan, but of course it had not helped her to believe they were being pursued by an enemy.

She led him into the great hall. A burly and impassive servant took care of their luggage, walked it away. She gave him a moment to look around, then conducted him on into the receiving room, where he went three steps, before slowing as he saw the welcoming committee. Steeling himself to be calm, he put on a stiff smile and nodded as Sarah introduced him.

'Uncle Mike, this is Napoleon Solo. We met at the convention. He's very interested in your process. He's been telling me all—' Her chatter faltered as she suddenly sensed the electric atmosphere of the room.

Trilli and his men were rigid, explosively ready at the

first sound of his name. Solo felt wound-up like a watch-spring. He hadn't counted on walking flat-footed right into the middle of this gang. One false move now and the bomb would go off. The only relaxed ones in the room were O'Rourke himself and his black-haired bright-eyed niece. She produced a sizzling smile. O'Rourke made a lordly gesture. If he sensed the tension, he gave no sign of it.

'Be welcome to my little kingdom, Mr. Napoleon Solo. Sure and that's the fine brave name you have. An emperor – and a king. We're well met!'

'You're very kind. I ought to apologize for this intrusion.'

'Not at all. Sarah speaks for you, that's enough. In a moment I'll ask you to take a seat and be at home, for sure and you've travelled a long way and must be weary. But first, a small ceremony. On the table before you, you'll see a can of O'Brien's Beautiful Beer, the finest brew there is, known affectionately all over the world as 3-B. Am I speaking the truth, sir?'

Solo grinned. 'I won't argue with that. I've heard it very well spoken of.'

'A gentlemanly reply. Well now, seeing that this castle, which is my home, and all the sweet luxuries in life that I'm fortunate to own, all come directly from the sale of that beverage before you, I make it a custom to ask every guest of mine on his first visit to drink a ceremonial glass of it. Will you do that for me, now?'

Solo heard him, stared at the innocent can, and held back a frown. He missed Sarah's quick bewilderment at this brand new 'ceremony', as well as Bridget's hasty finger-on-lip gesture and wink to her as if to say it was all only a small jest.

'I wouldn't want to break an old custom,' he smiled, and picked up the can. It bore the familiar 3-B label and it was cold, little beads of condensation forming on the sides.

'We saw you coming up the road and laid it on special,' the old man explained as Solo applied the opener and poured beer into the glass. Solo raised the glass, sniffed without seeming to do so. It seemed all right. He sipped, tasted, swallowed, and it was very good indeed. Just right.

40

'Your very good health,' he said, nodding. 'This goes down well on a hot day like this.' It had a sharp clean flavour, with just the right touch of tangy bitterness. He sensed the tension receding a little. Trilli and his uglies were relaxing now, settling into their seats.

O'Rourke spoke again: 'You've not met my other niece, Bridget, have you?'

Solo bowed gravely. Hers was a different loveliness from that of Sarah's; she had an exotic flame-like quality, her dark tresses framing an exquisitely heart-shaped face. 'I'm very pleased to meet you,' he declared, with sincerity.

'Dr. Trilli, Mr. Foden, Mr. Schichi – my house-guests. And now we're all acquainted, won't you be seated and make yourself at home, Mr. Solo. Will you see after the tea, Bridget, and hurry it along.'

Solo watched her move away. Sheer poetry. And there had been a glint in her eye. Had it not been for the three uglies, he would have regarded this as a very promising situation. He cast an eye over the oil-paint ancestors and wondered, wryly, if this eccentric old man really believed he was royal. And what, oh what, was Trilli and that thick-skulled pair doing here? It wasn't like THRUSH to come boldly out into the open in this way.

'So you're interested in my process, then?' O'Rourke asked. 'You're a chemist?'

'Well, no. Not exactly. I only know what Miss Sarah has told me.' He gave her a smile, and lingered a moment to appreciate the picture she made as she smiled back. Again he toyed with the pleasant problem as to which was the lovelier, her or Bridget. 'So far as I can understand, you've made something of a breakthrough, a new technique and a new synthetic with some rare and unusual properties. Right?'

'That's a way of putting it. But if you're not a chemist, just what is your interest?'

'That would depend on the properties, wouldn't it?'

'That's very true. And wasn't I just this moment beginning to discuss that very thing with Dr. Trilli here?' He turned to address Trilli now. 'You'll have heard, I'm sure,

41

of a series of nerve gases the Allies were developing in the
last war. There was one, I recall, which destroyed a man's
nerve. Made him a coward. Remember? I see you do. A
dreadful thing, to be sure, and what a weapon to use against
an enemy! But did it ever strike you that the direct reverse
would be just as terrible?'

'What does this mean, reverse?' Trilli mumbled.

'That's one of the effects of the stuff I'm talking about. It
takes about five minutes to act. It takes away a man's caution, his sensible judgment. It inflates his confidence to an
enormous degree, gives him a head full of daring and courage, a complete lack of fear of any kind. Would you call
yourself a brave man, Mr. Solo?'

Solo shrugged, put his head on one side modestly and
smiled. 'I don't know. I suppose I'm as brave as most.' Inwardly he seethed with contempt. The doddering old fool!
King Mike, hah! And rabbity little four-eyes there, with
his hired musclemen. 'I don't scare easily, anyway,' he
offered.

'I'm sure you don't.' O'Rourke nodded gently and turned
to Trilli again. 'You see, courage without caution is nothing
more than foolhardy recklessness, and it can be deadly
dangerous. I'm sure Mr. Solo is a brave man. I'm sure if
this room were suddenly full of guns, all pointed at him and
all threatening sudden death, he wouldn't turn a hair.
Would you, Mr. Solo?'

'If you're trying to scare me, you're wasting your time!'
Solo laughed, with an obvious sneer now. He watched Trilli
draw a pistol, a vicious little snub-nosed automatic. Then
Foden waved one, and then Schichi. All he did was to laugh
again, calmly relaxed in his seat. 'Fumbling amateurs,' he
said scornfully. There was a sibilant rustle as the oil-paintings rolled back and he stared around at the massed array
of pointing shotguns. Still he smiled. 'Kid stuff! I can't
blame you too much, seeing that you don't know who I am,
but if you think this row of popguns is going to scare anybody you're all wrong! I could take on all of you, right now,
and not even work up a sweat.'

Faintly at the back of his mind, the small voice of sanity

42

screamed a warning to him – but he was in no mood to heed it. He felt good – ten feet tall at least. Odds like this were what brought out the real fire in a man. He turned a confident smile on Sarah, who was straining forward towards him with horror on her face.

'Don't you worry, honey,' he assured her. 'I've walked out of tougher spots than this before breakfast. Just let one of them start something, that's all.' He surveyed the grim faces mockingly. 'Just try me, that's all. Dr. O'Rourke, you don't seem to be aware of it, but you are entertaining three very lousy characters. Scum, that's what. THRUSH agents, in other words. They'd cut your throat and rob you blind, like that!' He snapped his fingers. 'Only they won't, not while I'm here.'

'Uncle!' Sarah turned to O'Rourke in shrill fear. 'What have you done to him?'

'Uncle!' Solo echoed, laughing. 'That's it. The man from U.N.C.L.E. That's me. Have no fear!' He saw O'Rourke's face undergo a subtle alteration, a quiet hardening. Sarah half-rose, but a chill voice came from behind her.

'Sit still and keep quiet!' It was Bridget, and there was menace in her tone. 'You too, Mr. Napoleon Solo. Just sit very still!' He felt the cold muzzle of a weapon pressed against the side of his head. 'The rest of you can put away your armament now – I'll take care of this. Carry on talking, Uncle Mike.'

But Trilli wanted to put in an objection. 'This is very interesting, but is still only talk. He sounds foolishly arrogant, true. But is this all? What about actions, other symptoms? Is he drunk? Does it show? Can it be detected?'

'All taken care of, Dr. Trilli,' O'Rourke said calmly. 'There are no symptoms other than a slowdown of reaction-times. He is cold sober, by any test – on one glass of beer, what else would you expect? And there isn't a chemist in the world would find anything suspicious, either in the beer or his bloodstream . . . not unless he knew exactly what to look for, and possibly not even then.'

Solo heard him, but his attention remained on the vanishing guns, as he weighed the odds against him. O'Rourke sm: d at him. 'You're in the enemy camp, Mr. Solo. You must realize that by now. But it won't worry you, of course!'

Solo mind was now as clear as crystal. He gathered himself, sna ed a wink at Sarah, and exploded into furious action. On hand snaked up and back to snatch Bridget's gun, the oth dived into his coat to whip out his own. Sheer expert speed we him the advantage, he thought – only, for some weird r ason, it did not work out like that.

His arms seem d to be ploughing through syrup, and while he was fighti · the sluggishness, Bridget leaned over, twisted his own gu from his grasp, and thumped him savagely alongside the emple with the butt of the one she held. Stars flared painful in his skull.

'As you see,' O'Rourk pointed out with clinical calm, 'his reaction-times are dep ssed in inverse ratio to the enhancement of his confidence.'

Solo shook his head, furiously angry at this setback, regretting the loss of his gun but unshaken in his determination. What was a gun, anyway? In the old days in Korea there hadn't been one man in the whole outfit with the nerve to take him on at unarmed combat. He lurched to his feet, ducking away from Bridget, who stood back to let him go.

'All right, now!' he snarled. 'The game is over, folks—'

'Napoleon!' Sarah wailed, half-rising again to put out a hand to him as he backed up against the wall. 'What's come over you?'

Her uncle snarled at her in sudden sharp anger: 'Keep quiet, woman! Can you not see this is a scientific experiment? Mr. Foden, perhaps you would be kind enough to give us a little bit more proof?'

'A pleasure!' Foden grinned, showing his teeth, and rose to move around the table. Watching him advance, Solo fell into a tense crouch. He ached with rage and the eagerness to blow off some of it. This thick-headed Nazi type would serve that purpose admirably.

Solo smiled thinly. 'I can lick any THRUSH in the house,' he said mockingly.

Foden came close, hunched his shoulders to toss a punch

44

– and again the deadly sluggishness got in the way as Solo put up an arm to ward it off. The punch got through, smashed him back against the wall. He struggled in futility, and another roundhouse wallop rocked him, making bells clang in his head. It was like a bad dream, only the solidity of those flailing fists was painfully real and he could do nothing to stop them. Through a darkening haze he saw Foden reach out carelessly, setting him up with a left, with a murderous right to follow – and it hurt, and he couldn't seem to get his arms to cooperate fast enough. His legs softened, only the hard wall at his back serving to hold him up. Out of the awful nightmare he heard O'Rourke's old voice in sharp command:

'That'll do for now, me bucko! Leave him be. We might have use for him later, maybe.' The punches stopped coming. Solo leaned gratefully on the wall and tried to shake the booming throb of agony out of his head.

'This man is an U.N.C.L.E. agent,' Trilli said. 'I have heard much of him. He is dangerous. We should destroy him at once.'

'I've heard of U.N.C.L.E. too, Dr. Trilli. Ye have no need to tell me what to do. Let me remind you, I am still the king of this castle, and I am no more afraid of U.N.C.L.E. than I am of THRUSH. He doesn't look so dangerous at this moment, you will allow? And I've a dungeon downstairs that will hold our Mr. Solo until I want him again. Will you lend a hand there, Mr. Foden, and bring him along this way?'

'Uncle Mike!' Sarah cried out, frantic now. 'You can't do this. These men are criminals and murderers! I won't let you do this!'

'Mr. Schichi, will you oblige me by keeping her quiet and bringing her along too,' said O'Rourke calmly. 'She's a clever girl in her way, but was always a bit of a nuisance with her high and mighty notions. She's served her purpose, I'm thinking. And we might be able to try another experiment with her. If you're interested, Dr. Trilli? No? This way then, boys!'

Solo staggered helplessly in Foden's harsh grip, his head

45

spinning and his legs uncertain. He was dimly aware of walking, of a dark doorway and spiral steps dropping downwards, the chill damp of stone walls, and noisy echoes.

'It was an extensive dungeon,' O'Rourke explained, 'until I had most of it converted to a laboratory and workshop. I kept a couple of the old cells to serve as storerooms. In here, Mr. Foden, if you would be so kind. Ah, wait a moment now.' Solo lifted his head blearily, to see the old white-bearded face close to his. 'I'm a man for doing things in style, Mr. Solo, although you might not think it. To all my distinguished guests, of whatever persuasion, I like to present my personal card. You, just the same as the rest!' And he felt the old man stuff something into his breast pocket. It seemed the final touch of insanity. Then Foden sent him reeling with a powerful thrust, and he staggered helplessly against a cold stone wall, Sarah being thrust in after him.

A very heavy and solid door thudded shut, found its echo in Solo's head, and silence followed. He leaned on the wall, pressed his brow against the cold stone, and tried to think. He heard Sarah sobbing helplessly. It was as if he were split right down the middle. Part of his mind told him he was in a desperate situation, that both of them were, but the other half still felt like a giant, a conquering hero, valiant and undeterred by his misfortunes. There was a stranger in his skull, a crazy man full of instant schemes to break down the door and bust out, sweeping all the opposition grandly aside. Thinking sanely with that demon in charge was a heavy task.

It must be the drug, he mused thickly. *And the drug must have been in the beer-can.* But he had opened it himself! You couldn't tamper with a thing like that, surely? He abandoned that problem for the moment, lifted his head from the cold stone and began sizing up the cell.

The available light was meagre, and with a greenish tint. It came from a small window high up on the wall, a window with stout bars and not big enough to let a boy through even with those removed. It must be at ground level, up there, judging by the rank grass that half-covered it to pro-

46

duce the greenish hue. The idiot in his head urged him to leap up, rip out the bars and force his way through. He made himself ignore the voice, but the devilish implications of the drug began to show themselves as he thought about it. The fine difference between confident courage and foolhardy recklessness is hard enough to judge in any case, and harder still to recognize in oneself. Given a drug to blur that line, the results could be terrifyingly lethal.

Who would suspect one pleasant can of 3-B as being the pathway to a swift death? Certainly not the bus-driver quenching his thirst, or an airline pilot, a motor-cyclist – or a window-cleaner, a construction worker on his scaffold, a welder, a blacksmith, an electrician – or a doctor performing a critical operation – a jay-walker— The list was virtually endless. Anyone and everyone needs the critical counterbalance of due care and caution. And one can of 3-B was enough to destroy this sense completely!

Solo groaned and rubbed his head as he considered the matter. O'Brien's Beautiful Beers was a massive concern. From that brewery out there millions of gallons of the stuff flowed in rivers to all parts of the English-speaking world. The old man hadn't been exaggerating when he had claimed to be able to bring the world to its knees.

Sarah's sobbing broke through his gloomy thoughts. He turned, to see her hunched against the door, slim and white in the gloom, looking more lovely and more vulnerable than ever in her shock and despair. He straightened up, feeling his mind gradually growing more clear, second by second.

'How much of this did you know?' he demanded, and she dropped her hands from her face to stare woefully at him.

'Nothing at all!' she wailed. 'Napoleon, I *told* you, I don't know about the drug's effects. You've got to believe me. I only work on the production side, the process. Making the stuff. And not very much of that, even. We made only a trial batch or two, until we could find some market for it. And that's all I know. That's the truth, so help me.'

'Hmm! Tell me, just how much of 3-B does your uncle own, if any?'

'Oh, just about all of it, I think. He's a cunning old man, you know, in his way. I've always known he was a bit – eccentric. But now! Napoleon – he's mad, isn't he?'

Solo nodded slowly, still hearing the irrational ghost in his own mind raging in fury and frustration. 'What was all that nonsense about giving me his card?' he asked.

'I don't know. I don't know anything at all, any more.' Her voice began to quaver now; she was like a child who had been slapped and was just realizing the fact.

Solo scowled to himself, and turned to peer about the narrow cell. Against the wall and just inside the door stood a cardboard carton. He stooped to check it. Cans of beer. It had been opened and a few were missing, but he could easily estimate the total number. Four by six – two dozen to a pack. A big and burning question came to mind.

'Surely the old fool isn't going to scatter this stuff indiscriminately? What would be the point in that? Where would he gain?'

She brushed a hand across her eyes to wipe tears away, then moved away from the door and came to stand beside him and look down. 'I don't know – I can't seem to think straight. The cans are a new idea, I know that.'

'What d'you mean, new?'

'Well, you've never seen 3-B in a can before, that I know. Because we have only just had the canning plant put in. It's a new line. And, so far, it is only for overseas. England, to start with.'

'You're sure about that?'

'Of course I am! No self-respecting God-fearing Irishman would ever drink beer out of a tin can! We had a market survey done, to be sure of it. So the first trial consignment will be for England.'

'*Will* be? You mean it hasn't gone yet? None?'

'Not so far as I know. Uncle said something about waiting for the right moment to hit the market. I don't know what he had in mind. I would have said, myself, that this weather was the perfect time—'

'I think I know!' Solo interrupted harshly. 'This is a mass

demonstration, all ready and standing by to convince THRUSH. First he had to get Trilli, or somebody like him, to show some interest, to let him see what the stuff can do. The next step is to stage a full-scale demonstration. And this is it. A bulk shipment to England.' He straightened up. 'How much would there be in a consignment?'

'Oh! I know that. Three lorry-loads, a thousand cartons to each.'

'Oh, brother!' he muttered. 'Six thousand dozen! Death by the truckload! I have got to stop that, somehow!'

'First we have to get out of here,' she said, suddenly practical.

'You have a point there,' he agreed. He moved to the door and examined it with practiced fingers and a keen eye. He felt himself again. The faint light was going fast. The window was hopeless. And so, too, was the door – he had to admit it after a hard examination. Apparently the feudal Irish had not believed in locks, keyholes or any other kind of openings, for there wasn't a break of any kind in the solid oak planking. Even the hinges were safely established on the outside, where he couldn't get at them. He tried one futile savage thrust, enough to assure him that nothing short of a battering ram would shake that massive portal. He guessed it was secured on the outside by some form of bar-and-hasp arrangement.

He went back to the carton, took out a can, hefted it. It would make a serviceable club, or something to throw. At what? Cans of beer, full of dope to drive men mad. Six thousand dozen! Hopeless. He dropped it, went back to where she stood by the door.

'What are we going to do?' she asked softly.

'We are going to count on the fact that your uncle is a man who believes in doing a thing with style. That, therefore, he will remember and want to feed us. To do that, somebody has to come through that door. And that's our only chance, so we have to make the most of it.'

'But – we're not armed!'

'We have our brains,' Solo said, and wondered briefly if this were just another brag caused by the fading drug in

49

his bloodstream. Then he mentally shrugged – he felt normal enough now, and he didn't have time to question each of his thoughts. Decisively, he said, 'Let me have your stockings, will you?'

'What do you want them for?'

'Sarah, dear, I can't help pointing out that you have a bad habit of talking too much. You'll have to get over that. Now be quiet and listen while I explain. And listen carefully, because this has to be done just right!'

CHAPTER THREE

'LOVELY NIGHT FOR A DRIVE, ISN'T IT?'

THE little pick-up truck stood just off the road, securely hidden by thick bushes blazing with wild red roses. Illya Kuryakin sat at the wheel and watched the purple sunset darken into dusk. The warm air was rich with smells and the quiet peace of eventide. Part of his mind appreciated the surrounding beauty, but most of his attention was checking back over everything he had done, just to make sure. He had surveyed Cooraclare Castle from every possible vantage point. He had studied diagrams and sketches until he knew by heart every wall and room in that stone fort. Of one thing he was sure. The original builders had designed the place to be difficult to get into, and they had succeeded. The only official way in was through the massive main gate into the forecourt, and he had no intention whatever of trying that route. Careful questions and a bit of judicious gossip had taught him that the place was well-stocked with men, with crude but effective armament.

He watched the light fade, and reflected on his own chosen methods. He wore a lightweight and neat suit of tough black whipcord, its rather bulky outlines due to the varied assortment of equipment he had stowed away about his person. Over it all, now, he was going to fit something else. From a dashboard pocket he drew out a slim flat pack

50

which unfolded into a two-piece affair of thin black stretch-plastic, tough and waterproof.

When he had squirmed into this protective skin he began moving away from the truck, up the road, slipping a close-fitting black cap over his straw-blond hair. The sheer stuff hugged him tight, made sure there would be no projecting awkwardnesses to trap him. He was a slim black shadow as he crossed the road and came to a low stone bridge over a stream. He slid down the bankside like a cat, ducked under the stone arch, and touched the pencil-beam on his wrist. The spot of light searched and found the yawning black hole he had known would be there.

This was the main drain outlet from the castle, a generous four-foot pipe. He blessed O'Rourke's scientific forethought in wanting a really serviceable drain. He had studied this pipe-system at great length in the drawings. Now he ducked and went crawling in, gauging his progress with great care, the fine beam continuously searching ahead.

Odd and irregular gushes of water came along the bottom of the pipe to meet him.

After half an hour of steady travel he came to the first of a series of smaller inlets, stumps of lead piping that dripped or poured. He went more cautiously now, comparing the scene with what he had in his memory. Ahead of him a pipe suddenly gushed vaporous hot water which had a pleasant perfume to it. Somebody had just finished taking a bath. He stopped, let the flood go by, and drew out from his store a small contact-microphone and earpiece.

He lay still and listened. Then he stirred, moved on, and listened again. Nothing but random clicks and bumps, so far. He moved on, shifting the microphone from one spot to another on the glaze of the pipe over his head. All at once he froze and kept very still as he heard footsteps. They were very near. He searched with the beam and saw another pipe, larger than the rest, which led straight down into the main. He knew exactly where he was now. He kept still, listening. He heard voices, quite plainly:

51

'—is the prototype plant only, of course. A bench model. The full-scale equipment is in the new wing of my laboratory, over at the brewery. I'll be letting you take a look at that tomorrow.'

'So. Dr. O'Rourke, besides yourself, how many people know the full details of this process?'

'Not a one, Dr. Trilli, not a one! Various people know various bits and pieces, to be sure, but I'm the only one that knows the whole thing. I'm sure you'll appreciate the wisdom of that, eh? Well now, if you've seen enough, I think it's time we went and had supper—' The voices went away.

Kuryakin nodded to himself. Right under the dungeon laboratory, just as he had calculated. He put away the microphone and earpiece and got out a slim tool with a diamond tip.

Spurts of dust and glittering specks of glaze hung in the air as he scored a deep line in the glaze of the pipe until he was through to the stone-grit below. Patiently and steadily he cut another line, then another, until he had made a cambered square. When he was satisfied, he put away the cutter, drew off his shoe, braced himself, and struck a hard, precise blow upwards. Then a quick traverse along the breaks with a slim chisel, and a curved section of pipe fell into his waiting hands. Dirt dribbled for a moment, then he set to work with the chisel again. He struck the close-matched edges of floor-tiles, prized one up and away, then another, making a hole. Soon it was big enough to pass his shoulders. He went up through, touching the underside of a bench with his hand, grasping and hauling himself clear.

With no change whatever in his seriously intent expression, he sent the pencil-beam of light winking around the laboratory and saw that it was well-appointed. A glance told him that much, enabled him to identify much of the equipment. Centrifuge, evaporator, distillation flasks, a balance chromatograph column, an oscilloscope – and a row of cans of 3-B. He raised an eybrow at those.

Then the beam picked up something much more interesting. On the floor beside a tall filing cabinet stood a heavy

52

old-fashioned steel safe. He went across and crouched down to study it, then turned to scan the laboratory again. He tried a drawer or two in the cabinet. All free and open. Everything out in the open – except this safe. This, therefore, would be where the valuable stuff was, if any. The secrets. He tapped the thing with a gloved hand and saw that it wouldn't be too hard to break into.

He groped into pockets, hauled out a close-rolled strip of putty-like plastic explosive, pinched off a length and stuffed it delicately into the small gaps by the hinges of the door. He worked swiftly and with total concentration. It had to be done just right. Slim wires and a detonator went into place.

He glanced around and caught up a couple of small cushions from the laboratory seats, took a white dust-coat from its hook on the inside of the laboratory door, rolled the lot into a thick pad, patting and folding. He pressed the pad into place, set his back to it and crouched to hold it in place, leaning against it.

He held a bared wire, touched it to a contact, and there came a dull thump, a muffled blow that pitched him forward to his knees. He scrambled up immediately and whirled around to slap at the smouldering cloth and put it out. Then he braced himself and lifted the heavy door clear, carefully pushing it aside.

The dancing light showed him a few casual papers, nothing important, a small clutch of bottles and boxes – and a flat, black-bound notebook. He grabbed that, crouched and let the light shine on the pages as he flipped them. Molecular diagrams. He read a few hurried words, flipped another page and saw a flow-diagram schematic of a process. This was it, he decided.

He was stuffing the book safely away when his alert ear caught the tramp of footsteps coming near. He killed his light instantly, drew out a pistol, and crept quickly to the laboratory door, listening intently. The steps came closer, were on stone, echoing.

He readied himself, easing back. There was an odd jinking clatter, as if someone carried a tray with plates and cups.

The pistol levelled in his grip. The steps grew very loud, and went steadily on past the door.

Frowning, he tried the handle and eased it open just a crack, then wider, and squinted out. The passage outside was stone-floored and garishly lit with a row of naked bulbs in the vaulted roof, bright enough to reveal Schichi with a tray.

He was setting it down now, grunting as he stooped, setting it beside a massive wooden door. Then he stepped cautiously back, pulled out a gun and spoke loudly.

'You in there! I'm going to loosen the door. You wanna eat, you gotta come and get it!' Then he ducked forward, grabbed the massive beam that held the door fast, slid it noisily along, beat once with his fist, and ducked back again. 'All right, now!' he called again. 'Come on out real slow!'

There came no sound, no move, no response at all. Kuryakin watched curiously as Schichi fidgeted and frowned and then ducked forward again, holding his gun ready, to seize the door and heave – and jump back. The heavy door creaked slowly open. Schichi raised his voice.

'Come on, now, cut the comedy! You want grub – *Hey! What the hell!*' His voice sharpened in sudden astonishment and he went charging in through the door. Kuryakin, moving like a cat, whipped along the passage to watch, heard him take three heavy steps, and then there was a grunt and the thud of a vicious blow. Schichi went down flat on his face, and the man who had chopped him from ambush against the wall now made a frantic snatch and seized the gun from the limp hand as it fell.

Kuryakin saw that. He could see over the crouching figures of the two combatants, into the cell and over to the far wall, where, from the thick bars of a tiny window, hung the hideously limp shape of a girl, her head twisted to one side, the silk stocking around her throat stretching up to the bars. Hanged by the neck! Kuryakin's steely gaze dropped again to the man who was now straightening, gripping the gun, spinning.

'Hello, Napoleon,' he said mildly. 'I've always thought

you were a lady-killer, but this is a bit extreme, isn't it?'

Solo stared, then relaxed with a crooked grin. 'It worked, though, didn't it? And it's not as bad as it looks, at that.' He spun around and went over to the wall. 'It's all right, honey, all over. Hold still a moment – there, you can come down now.' The 'dead' girl shook her hair from her face, slid out of the belt that had held her under the arm-pits, released the twisted stockings from her throat and left them dangling from the window-bars. Solo took his belt and slung it around his waist.

The girl looked down at Schichi with a shudder, then her eyes fell on the new arrival and she caught her hand to her mouth. 'Who – who's that?' she quavered.

'That's my odd-job man, honey. Illya Kuryakin – Sarah O'Rourke.'

'I hope you're not as bloody-minded as your cousin Bridget,' Illya murmured, inclining his head a fraction. 'Is she, Napoleon?'

'Not this one. King Mike was saving the pair of us for a few of his gruesome experiments. She's on our side. How'd you get in here?'

'Up through the laboratory floor. It seemed the easiest way. Do you have anything to linger for?'

'Not a thing, and this place is stuffed tight with Irish shotgunners. Let's get out of here, fast!'

'What about the Mafia here?'

'He can snore in our place. It won't hurt him any.' Solo slid the tray inside with a foot, swung the door shut and shoved the bar across. 'That's that. Lead on!'

They hurried into the laboratory, where Illya showed them the hole under the bench. 'Goes down into the drain and then along for half a mile. You go ahead; I want to leave a farewell gift. I'll be right after you.'

He watched them disappear, then began fumbling out more gear. A small but heavy box went up against the door. The rest of the plastic explosive was packed around it. Wires. A tiny timing mechanism which he set by his watch. He moved now, on an afterthought picking up one of the

55

cans of beer. Then he slid swiftly down into the hole and flashed his light ahead. Solo and Sarah were well away, and they all scrambled faster with the aid of the light. He caught up to them as they stumbled out into the cool night under the small bridge. The stream gurgled quietly beneath them. The air was pleasant on their warm faces.

'Just over a minute,' Illya estimated, holding his watch steady, seeing the seconds tick away. There came a sullen rumble and a great drumming blast of air along the pipe, a shock through the ground, and a distant roar in the air. 'It was only a small bomb,' he said regretfully. 'Not enough to blow up a whole castle. But it will ruin the laboratory and puzzle them a bit.'

'I feel a lot better just for that,' Solo said. 'Better still when I see that yon Italian lunkhead had at least the good sense to bring back my own gun. We'd better travel, Illya. How are we fixed for mobility?'

'I've a small pick-up about five minutes' walk down this road. Come on. Anybody got an opener, by the way?' He flourished the beer-can, and Solo snatched it from him with a stifled curse, tossed it into the stream and took aim on it. The pistol coughed in his hand, and there came a *plunk* from the can.

'Not for you, old man,' he said. 'I'll explain in a minute. First – can you locate the brewery from here?'

'I think so. Urgent?'

'Very much. Six thousand dozen cans of 3-B are due to ship out any time now, overland. We have to stop that shipment, somehow.'

'You haven't suddenly gone Prohibitionist, have you, Napoleon? I can't blame you for not feeling affectionate towards King Mike, but that's no reason to knock his beer, is it?'

'You don't know what's in the stuff,' Solo growled. 'All the beer in those cans is doped with Mike's molecules.' He went on to fill in the background and his own reasoning as they scrambled up the bankside and across the road. Kuryakin listened intently, and nodded.

'Sounds logical,' he agreed. 'Have you any idea just what

56

the stuff does? I had word from U.N.C.L.E. One, but just the hint that it could be a hallucinogen. That's vague enough. Do you know anything more?'

'Plenty!' Solo retorted, with feeling. 'This is one of the best. It's nothing more nor less than canned courage exaggerated out of all reason. King Mike tried one on me without warning. It's dynamite!' He went on to describe and catalogue his 'symptoms' as clearly as he could, trying to be objective about them, stressing the fact that he had felt perfectly normal at the time.

'You're quite sure you weren't drunk?'

'On one can of beer? Slightly less than half a pint? What do you think? But I felt like a regiment of giants eager and willing to take on the Chinese menace all by myself. I could have walked through walls. In actual fact' – he grinned ruefully – 'I was slowed up so much that Foden was hitting me whenever and however he wanted to.'

They reached the truck and Kuryakin slid into the driving seat, Sarah scrambled in beside him, and Solo got in last of all, slamming the door shut. And then he snorted in a way that made Kuryakin look at him critically and ask, 'Something on your mind, Napoleon?'

'Yeah. The dope is finally wearing off, and the pattern has sprung a few stitches. Try this for size, Illya. King Mike is no fool, but a crafty old planner. He is about to ship six thousand dozen cans of doped beer to be transported to England. We know what that stuff can do. We can imagine what the result will be. I will even allow that this is a mass demonstration put on by the old man to show THRUSH his muscles. But—'

'But what?'

'Think what's going to happen next. Death and disaster on a large and shocking scale, right? Then the law starts to check back. What's their first question in an auto accident, say, or any kind of accident that seems to be caused by recklessness? "Was he drinking?" And, sooner or later, they're going to tie in the coincidences, and pin the blame right on 3-B. Which means that Mike is in trouble. At the least, financial ruin. At worst, multiple manslaughter. Of course, most of the damage will be done by then, but all the same, it's sloppy thinking on his part. Or is it?'

'On the contrary.' Kuryakin smiled slightly as he stared out into the dark. 'It's actually very crafty psychology on the old man's part. I was on a job in England just recently. They are currently very concerned about drunken driving. and working on some efficient way of telling whether a man is drunk or not. You'd never convince them that one can of beer would have any effect on a man. They just wouldn't believe it.'

'And Uncle Mike did say,' Sarah offered, 'that no chemist would ever be able to detect anything amiss, either in the man or the beer!'

'That I can believe,' Kuryakin nodded. 'Fractional traces are hard to find, even when you know what to look for. Interesting stuff.' He glanced at Solo. 'I wonder how it would affect somone who's *not* naturally conceited?'

'What's in the back of the truck?' Solo asked, ignoring the gibe.

'Portable generator and assorted items of mayhem.' They moved off and gathered speed. 'You never know what you might need, to get into a castle.' They rolled on a while in amicable silence, these two who were so unlike in temperament yet so close in spirit. Sarah sat shivering between them, even now hardly able to believe the nightmare was over for a while.

'Do you think,' she asked quietly, 'that Uncle Mike actually had it in mind to kill me?'

'We'll never know that,' Napoleon said. 'And, for my part, I'd just as soon leave it that way. One thing's certain. He intends to kill a whole lot of people with that beer shipment unless we can figure out some way to stop it.' They came to a low crest and he called gently, 'Hold it, Illya. . . . Isn't that the brewery down there, Sarah?'

They were looking down over a great square space filled with orderly blocks of buildings, all neat and functional. Most of it lay in darkness, but there was one corner where lights burned and people moved about their business. She stared down.

'That's it,' she declared. 'And there's something going on. That's the loading gate, there. And the lorries, see?'

'Get going!' Solo snapped, and the little truck roared into speed down the gentle slope. The large black masses had triggered off an instant and ghastly suspicion in his mind. The beer was being loaded up right now. Headlights stabbed at them from a bend, and Kuryakin hauled the truck over to hug the roadside as a small van went roaring past in the other direction.

'What will you bet,' he offered mildly, 'that they're on their way to help out at the castle?'

'Rescue operations? It could be. We might be able to use that idea.' The truck hit the flat now and roared around a bend, to pull into a long straight road that lay alongside a high wire and steel fence. On ahead they saw the red warning of tail-lights which were moving.

'What will *you* bet,' Solo said, 'that there goes our precious shipment of death? After 'em, Illya!'

'With what?' the practical Russian replied. 'We might be able to catch them, it's true. But then what?'

'You have a better idea?'

'Possibly. Miss O'Rourke, do you know anything about the laboratory work, the processing?'

'Yes, I do. Why?'

'Do you use homogenizing equipment? Ultrasonic agitators, to be more specific?'

'That's right. The latest—'

'We'll have to take a gamble, Napoleon; it's our only chance. We need that equipment. Miss O'Rourke, can you keep the gatekeeper talking while we roll past and in? Tell him anything you like, but we have to get in there.'

'All right, I'll try,' she promised, and scrambled past Solo as the truck neared the gate. 'The laboratory is away to your left as you get through,' she called, and eased the door open. Kuryakin trod on the brake, hauled the wheel around hard, nosing the truck through the still-open gate, slowing to let her drop off, then speeding up and swinging away to the left, to run alongside a long low building that was almost all glass in front. He braked to a stop and leaped out.

59

'I hope she remembers to bring the keys,' he muttered as they ran to the door. Solo went along, trusting his companion enough not to argue, but curious to know what he intended to do.

'What have you got in mind, Illya? Ultrasonic agitators?'

'You said six thousand dozen, Napoleon. You shot a hole in the can you took from me. Why? Because it's not enough to stop those trucks, or to run them off the road, even if we could. Ah, here she comes, *and* with the keys. Smart girl!'

Sarah came running, a slim black shape in the gloom, keys clinking in her hand. As the door opened she flicked on the lights and they all blinked at the myriad reflections from the gleaming chrome-work around them.

'Very neat!' Kuryakin approved, as they hastened into the fermentation room. 'Very neat indeed. And there's the fellow we want, right there.' He laid expert hands on the squat steel bulk of a cannon-shaped device that stood on a stubby plinth, its muzzle buried in the side of a huge vat. He began to wrench at wing-nuts.

'I'll disconnect the power-line!' Sarah gasped. 'Will you be able to manage? It's heavy!' Solo caught the idea of what was needed and got busy on the wing-nuts of the opposite side.

'Stir things up a bit, eh?' he grinned.

'Right!' Kuryakin grunted. 'This is used to agitate the brew, to speed up fermentation, aging, and to ensure perfect blending. Free on your side? Watch out for the weight now. How's the cable?'

Sarah came hurrying with the freed end, to pass it under and loop it as the two men hoisted the heavy unit.

'Make it double,' Kuryakin suggested, 'and we can use it as a carrier. That's it. Fine. Let it down easy, Napoleon. Now, if we grab the loops—'

They grunted and heaved, and she ran on ahead to hold doors open for them as they waddled with the massive thing between them.

'Can you drive?' Kuryakin asked the girl. She nodded hurriedly, and he smiled. 'Good – then hop into the driver's seat. Start up as soon as we're aboard. We'll be fixing this as we go.' They shambled out after her and laboured to heave the thing into the back of the truck, then scrambled in. She gunned the motor instantly, swinging the truck around in a tight curve.

'Where d'you want it?' Solo panted. 'Up on the roof of the cab?'

'Seems the best place. Let me free the cable first. Now – hup!' The two men groaned as they heaved the massive unit shoulder-high and slid it onto the cab-roof.

The truck roared along to the gate and went into another sharp turn, sending the glittering mass of steel skidding perilously. Solo grabbed for it, flipped a nonchalant hand to the goggling gatekeeper and called out, 'Much obliged. Good night!'

The truck swooped again in the opposite direction, into the road. Solo clung tight as the unit teetered. Kuryakin took the cable-end and went down on his knees beside the generator to wire up. It was a nightmare job, with only the narrow light of his wrist-light, the truck bouncing and swaying along the road, but he stuck at it patiently until all was secure. He spent a few precious moments making sure the generator was all ready to start up at the touch of a button, then straightened up and turned his face into the welcome coolness of the breeze.

Solo, clinging grimly to the precious unit, offered a heartfelt prayer that Sarah knew the route the beer-trucks would take. By the time Kuryakin stood up and announced that all was ready the little truck had cleared Conway and was snarling along the Ennis bypass, heading for Clarecastle and points southwest. To the right, between occasional clumps of trees, they could see the distant lights of Shannon airport. Kuryakin laid his hand on the agitator, took some of the weight and played his flashlight on it.

'How do you intend to aim and fire the thing?' Solo asked, curiously.

'By guess, I'm afraid. It isn't intended to be aimed, you know. This, see, is the frequency-setting. We can wind that up a bit. The more energy the better. And this is the focal

61

range. I'll set that as far out as it will go. According to the dial, that's twenty-five feet. And that's all we can do. No point in starting up the power until we see the trucks.'

'I think I've got it,' Solo murmured, 'but check me, just to make sure. The ultrasonic beam will stir up the beer in the cans, right?'

'Right! They are already under slight pressure. When the sonic beam hits, its energy will be transferred to the liquid, making it boil violently.'

'Should be fun!' Solo peered ahead, but the road as far as he could see was still deserted. They had cleared New-market On Fergus and were coming up fast on Hurler's Cross. He glanced at his watch. Just about midnight – and the whole place was deserted, quietly asleep. If this had been New York now . . .

'Those trucks are making fast time,' he muttered. 'We'll never catch them at this rate. Can you handle this on your own a bit?'

'I think so.'

'Good – let's see what I can do to speed things up a bit!' He hoisted up onto the cab and squirmed to lower his face over the side, to call into the open window. 'Get ready to move over, I'm coming down!' Then he changed ends, lowered his feet cautiously, slid them inside and went down in time to a convenient lurch of the truck. Sarah moved away, letting him grab the wheel. The noise of the motor fell off momentarily, then howled into new fury as he put his foot down hard. He gave her a quick reassuring grin and she tried hard to smile back.

'I daren't think,' she confessed. 'If I did I should be scared stiff!'

'Perfectly all right – we all get scared at times. It's a very useful feeling. That's what's so deadly about your uncle's molecules.'

'That was awful!' She shuddered. 'You looked – crazy – and helpless – at the same time. I thought you were going to be killed.'

'That bit bothers me.' He frowned, watching the road. 'I

gathered there were to be other experiments. Just how many trick synthetics has King Mike got, anyway?'

She shook her head in wonder. 'Only two that I know about. One's almost a mirror-image of the other – the structure-diagram, I mean. But the properties seem to be completely different, from the little I've heard. It's a fast-acting fermenting colloid.'

'Which means?'

'Well, when in contact with water it ferments very quickly and then sets into a thick jelly. Something the way starch does when you boil it.'

Solo shrugged. 'That doesn't sound so terrible, at any rate.'

Directly over his head, Illya Kuryakin would have disagreed had he been able to hear. That unshakably serious young man had hoisted himself onto the cab-roof, and with one arm wrapped around the ultrasonic unit he was playing the beam of his flashlight over that black-bound notebook in his other hand, and studying it with intense interest. There were some very intriguing diagrams in it, and the neatly written explanations were even more interesting.

' "At a liquid temperature of 60° F," ' he read, ' " the original sample ferments in a yeast-like manner, entraps water, doubling in volume every fifteen seconds for the first hour. The volumetric increase then falls off steadily, becoming stable after eight hours, when a colloidal suspension forms and the entire mass becomes extremely viscous. . . ." ' He flipped a page or two and came across one more diagram, an electronic lay-out this time. He studied it carefully as the truck jolted and swayed beneath him.

'Limerick!' Sarah peered ahead. 'The lorries will have had to slow down a bit, here. 'Tis a bit of a job to get through the cross-streets to the T 13, which they will have to do, you see, to make for Clonmel and then on to the road to Waterford and the boat.'

'Good!' Solo nodded. 'You'll have to pilot me here.' The black bulks of buildings began to rear up on either side of the road. Cobbles jarred them. He hauled on the wheel, swinging and whirling the truck crazily in response to her directions. They roared over Thomond Bridge, and he snatched a glance at the docks and long lines of shipping.

'Why don't you ship your stuff from here?' he wondered.

'We do!' she declared. 'But not to England. For that market it's quicker to run overland to Waterford and take the short sea-route. Whist now – I think that's them on ahead, see?'

Solo peered, then raised one hand from the wheel to thump on the roof over his head, grinning as a thump at once responded. Over the booming roar of the truck's motor he heard a sudden new growl and shudder, and knew that the generator was spinning.

He fastened his gaze on the winking tail-lights ahead, and cut his own headlights, leaving only the running lights glowing. They stormed through a clutter of cottages, a little backwater on the edge of town, and then out into the open again. The truck ahead drew near and he could see the tailboard and the narrow slats that held the shuddering cargo of cartons. Coming up fast. He tensed, remembering what Illya had said about a twenty-five foot range. He wondered if the driver ahead would have the common road courtesy to pull over to let him pass. Not that he was going to, not yet. Closer still. He eased his foot from the gas, peering ahead, waiting.

All at once the top left-hand carton flew apart in a bursting spout of amber froth, a wild succession of squirting jets of foam. His windshield grew a thick haze and he hit the wiper-switch frantically. He saw the next carton erupt in a firecracker series of spouting jets, and then the next. The heavy smell of beer flooded the cabin and foam piled up against the wiper-blades as the cartons vomited into destruction one after another.

On the roof of the cab Illya squinted against a rain of suds and relentlessly trained the whining unit along the top row of cartons, watching them burst into glorious ruin. Then he lowered his sights a fraction and swung back the reverse way. He felt the truck skid greasily as it ran into dribbling foam, and heaved madly to keep his aim. Solo fought the wheel like a madman, sensing that the driver ahead had noticed the trouble and was slowing down. He matched speeds instinctively and stared in awed fascination at the incredible carnage ahead – carton after carton bursting into a billowing mass of foam and spray, yellow beer spouting into the air from a dozen different directions at once.

The truck ahead slowed to a crawl and stopped. Solo matched it, but felt his rear wheels slip and the tail end of the truck slide over into the grass on the edge of the road. Now that his motor was idling he could hear the shrill scream of the ultrasonic unit over his head, with the steadily repeating *boff – boff – boff* as beer-cans ruptured under the lash of that energy-beam. His wipers clacked. The rear of the beer-truck was a yellow Niagara of foam now, with cartons still erupting crazily.

Solo saw the bewildered driver come hurrying around the tail-board of his truck, waving in futility at the rain of foam. In his hurry he ran right into a thick and sluggish stream of froth, lost his footing and went down with a mad flail of arms and legs. His co-driver came, cursing, from the other side, to slither and join his mate in the surging foam.

The can cannonade came to an abrupt halt, and there was a hard thump from the roof. Solo let in his clutch with delicate care, felt his wheels spin crazily for a moment and then take hold, and they were off again. He pressed his foot down on the gas, spun the wheel, and turned to grin at Sarah.

'One down, two to go, eh?'

She laughed crazily. 'Life is going to seem awfully dull after this!'

He felt a sudden qualm, a twinge of danger. 'Something we forgot,' he muttered. 'This damned stuff is potent, and who should know better than me? Try not to swallow too much of it!' She put her hand to her mouth in consternation. He groped in his breast pocket and got his handkerchief. 'Here! Make a mask of that and stick it over your face!'

She stared at the square of linen, then at the windshield, where drying froth was caking and blowing away in the breeze, and then at him.

'No!' she declared. 'You'd better have it. You're driving!' And she laid it on her knee and folded it with quick movements into a triangle. She was right, too. He set his jaw and held still as she placed the cloth over his nose and mouth and knotted the ends at his neck.

He thought of Illya, up on top and out in the open, without even the cab to partly shelter him. But he needn't have been worried. That calmly resourceful mind had already seen the danger, and more.

Solo grinned as he saw Illya's head, inverted, crane down from the roof to peer into the cab and shout through his masking handkerchief, 'That wasn't such a good idea, Napoleon. When we catch the next one I'll burst his tyres first, and then we won't have to run into the spray following him. Right?'

'Right!' Solo made a fist and a thumb-up gesture. 'I'd better be ready to stop fast, eh?' He drove his foot down now and they roared on through the dreaming countryside. They caught up with the second truck as it growled and snarled its way up a gentle rise just beyond a village that Sarah identified as Boher. Solo sent the truck sailing up after it, alert and ready to stamp on his brakes as the rear right wheel blew out with a report like a cannon, echoed in a fraction of a second by its companion on the left. The truck bounced to an abrupt halt. Solo hauled on the parking-brake, threw open the door.

'Stand by,' he warned, 'and watch my signals. I'm going to keep the truck crew diverted awhile.' He dropped and ran, hearing the first fusillade of bursting cans as he came up to the cab of the beer-truck. Putting on a wide-eyed innocent expression he stared up at the face which gave him a puzzled Irish frown.

'You have a couple of flats back there,' he said, 'What happened?'

66

'It sounded like a couple of punctures to me,' the driver argued.

'That's what I said. Flats. Blowouts. You call them punctures?'

'That's right, punctures. Is that what it was? Hell, for a minute there I thought me back-end had dropped out. D'ye hear that, Barney? The back tyres are gone! Only this morning I was telling Muldoon we should have had new ones this trip!'

Barney scratched his head in doubt. 'That doesn't sound like punctures to me,' he said. 'More like a machine-gun, I'm thinking. There now!' he said as another row of cartons erupted, 'did ye hear that? There's somebody taking shots at us, if you ask me!'

Beer fumes eddied on the air. Solo hoisted his make-shift mask, drew his pistol and backed away carefully. The driver's eyes popped.

'Hey!' he cried, all at once. 'Somebody's pinching the beer! I can smell it!'

Solo waved the pistol gently. 'Just sit still,' he advised, 'and you'll be all right. Nothing to be excited about.' He backed off still more, flicking a glance to see a spouting yellow cascade boil up in the back of the truck and surge in great lazy suds over the sides, while squirting volcanic jets leaped high in the air as Illya swept his weapon with cold efficiency. 'Fourth of July was never like this!' he mused as the last of the cartons blew apart into oblivion. He hooked a 'come on' gesture to Sarah, and the little truck stirred and came purring towards him.

He smiled at the astonished crew. 'Nasty stuff, canned beer. Better stick to the bottled stuff next time – it's safer. Good night!' He waved cheerily and caught the cab door as the truck went by. On impulse he used the momentum to swing him around, up and over into the back alongside Illya.

'That wasn't such a good idea either,' he frowned. 'If those two had been feeling nasty I'd have been in a spot. I couldn't very well shoot them.'

'That's right. We have to assume they're innocent parties. We might not be so fortunate with the last one.'

'Third time unlucky. It's a small miracle that truck didn't turn over, anyway. We'll have to cancel the blowout stunt.'

'We'll just have to choose a suitably wide stretch of road, pull alongside and keep pace, and get them that way.'

Solo nodded. 'All right. That's worth a try.' He grabbed for a handhold as the little truck lurched wildly across the road, straightened by a miracle and roared on again.

'I'm a fool!' he cried. 'We have a crazy woman at the wheel. She's been gulping the stuff down all this time! I'd better get back down there while we're still right side up!' He plunged for the roof, but Kuryakin tapped him on the shoulder and pointed ahead.

'Too late,' he said. 'There's our last pigeon now!'

'This road's wide enough, anyway. I'll give her a shout, tell her what to do. Let's hope she has sense enough to obey!' He clung and craned over at a perilous angle to peer into the cab and yell at her.

'Pull up alongside! Alongside! Keep even with him. Keep up the same speed – all right?'

'Yahoo!' she screamed back, her eyes afire. 'Down with the heathen blackguards! *Erin go bragh!*'

'And the best of luck to all of us,' he sighed, hauling himself back to stand beside his companion. 'Who was it who said, "Defend me from my friends; I can take care of my enemies myself"?'

'That was Voltaire. I agree with him. I would rather fight a dozen fools than have one on my side. Still – we will just have to bear with it.'

Illya hoisted himself up onto the cab-roof, to squat and haul the ultrasonic unit around to a broadside position. The little truck lurched and bucked as Sarah drove it madly on, rapidly overtaking the booming giant ahead.

'Pull out!' Solo prayed, biting his lip. 'For God's sake, Sarah, pull out!'

At the very last moment the little truck lurched violently sideways across the road, bumped into the ditch, swung back and came up alongside its prey. Now Solo stared in

68

awe as the cartons began to blow and burst in wild confusion, all over the place, top, bottom and sides, as Kuryakin struggled to keep aim against the crazy swaying and surgings of the little truck.

The chaos in the beer-truck was beyond description as cartons and cans alike danced and bubbled on streams of escaping beer, which spouted up, bobbing and leaping over a seething sea of froth, squirting like so many crazy ping-pong balls on a rifle range. They pulled up to hold level with the giant's cab. Solo waved to the driver.

'Lovely night for a drive, isn't it?'

The pleasantry got him a dark glare of suspicion. They fell back as Sarah trod a little too heavily on the brake. The beer-barrage went on. Solo could see, now, how the fine beam of sound carved its way through the froth and spray like an invisible knife. The poppings and splurtings died away.

Kuryakin made one last weary traverse, and said, 'I think that's all, Napoleon. Tell that madwoman we would like to go home now, would you?'

Solo craned himself over the edge of the cab once more to peer at her. 'Head for home, darling. It's all over. If you know another route, better take it. We won't be too popular where we've come from.'

She gave him a broad and dazzling smile. 'Do you know where we are right now? We're almost to Tipperary!'

'I've heard of it,' he admitted. 'It's a long way!'

'Not at all. Only a few more miles. Would ye like to go there?'

'Some other time. Let's go home, eh?'

'Home!' He saw the smile wash away from her face, leaving it crumpled and forlorn. 'I've no home left now. None at all.'

He realized instantly that what she said was absolutely true. More than that, he knew she was feeling the deadly letdown of the aftermath of the drug. He twisted his head around, to see that the last ruined beer-truck was now halted and falling behind.

'Pull in to the side and stop,' he ordered her, and swung

69

himself down as she obeyed. It took only a few strenuous minutes for the two men to drag the ultrasonic unit down from the cab-roof and stow it in the back of the truck.

Then Solo took the wheel. Sarah sat in between them, tears showing in her eyes as she reflected on her situation. Solo didn't feel too wonderful either as he put his foot down on the gas. Fast action was a fine thing for occupying the mind, but once it was over one's thoughts inexorably returned to the main problems and worried at them.

'You realize,' he said to Illya, 'that we've only postponed this thing for a while?'

'Yes, that's true. We still have to deal with King Mike and Trilli and his boys. And so long as they have the sense to stay put in Cooraclare Castle it will take an army to get them out.'

'We'll just have to scream for help.'

'But we won't get it, Napoleon. You're forgetting one thing. This is Eire. The Irish Free State. A republic!'

Solo gripped the wheel and stared grimly ahead, that simple reminder stirring his mind and making a lot of things suddenly fall into place. This little country, so peaceful on the surface, had a long and bitter history of fighting and feuding with England; Eire was independent and fiercely proud of it. There would be still many of the older generation with no love at all for Britain – and that would be why King Mike had directed his first murderous scheme against that nation.

Sarah began to weep silently, and he sympathized with her. All three of them were weary and hungry by now but Sarah herself had no home, no possessions and only the clothes on her back – plus the depressing after-effects of the drug to make her feel like death.

'Where are we?' he asked, to give her something positive to think about. 'I'm just going at random here.'

She knuckled her eyes, and Kuryakin unfastened his handkerchief and gave it to her. She thanked him, dabbed, and peered out as Solo slowed for a roadside signpost. A finger-post pointed back to Kilteely, another on to Herbertstown. She sniffed and pondered.

70

'We should strike a trunk road in a minute or two,' she said at last. 'If you turn right there, it will get us back to Limerick. It's the T 57.'

'That's for us, then. Perhaps the Limerick office will be able to come up with something. We'll see you safe, anyway.'

'If everything else fails,' Kuryakin observed, 'I have a very kind landlady in Ennis. I'm sure she can find you a room.' Silence fell over the trio for a moment as each retreated into his or her own thoughts. Kuryakin was frowning slightly, as though something were nagging at the back of his mind. Finally he said, 'Tell me, does your uncle dabble in electronics too? Radio gadgetry and that kind of thing?'

She gave one last dab with the handkerchief, handed it back to him and frowned in blue-eyed bewilderment.

'Not him. Whatever gave you that idea? I do, quite a bit. I like to mess about with gadgets and equipment. Why?'

'Just something I came across.' He fished out the enigmatic little notebook he had extracted from the safe and flipped the pages until he came to the curious circuit diagram. 'This. It seems to be a short-wave transmitter with a critically selective wave-length output.'

'That's mine!' She moved close to peer over his shoulder and point. 'Uncle Mike asked me to work this out, a long time ago. He didn't say what it was to be for, only that it had to put out a fine-tuned frequency, and to be adjustable – here, see?'

Solo shot a side-glance at the two heads close together and grinned wryly. In his serious and quietly intense way, Illya was something of a lady-killer himself. He certainly had Sarah's interest at this moment. Two technical minds together. Ah well, it was keeping her happy, if only for a little while. He paid attention to the road ahead. The total quietness and peace of this land caught at him. No wonder the children of Erin had been world-famous for philosophy and letters. This was a land in which a man would think, and take his time at it.

He slid into a semi-reverie in which he seemed to stand back and watch thoughts and ideas form and twist themselves into designs and patterns. Little by little a certain pattern stitched itself into shape, and it bothered him. He stirred, ran it through again, and it still bothered him. He sat up.

'Illya,' he murmured, in a deliberately casual tone. 'I've been thinking.'

'You can have fun like that, if you don't overdo it.'

'I've been thinking,' he repeated deliberately, 'what I would do, if I had been driving a truckload of beer peacefully through the night, and then, for no apparent reason, it suddenly blew itself all to pieces behind my back. And especially if I then saw a small pick-up truck go sailing by right after that.'

'What would you do?' Illya demanded.

'Well, I *think* I'd take a moment or two to gather my thoughts, but then I would hie me to the nearest telephone, and inform the place I had just departed from. Wouldn't you?'

'I suppose,' Illya agreed uneasily. 'That's if they have telephones!'

'We're not *that* backward!' Sarah cried. 'Of course we have the telephone!'

'Yes!' Solo stared thoughtfully at the long straight stretch of deserted road ahead. 'I sort of thought you had, somehow. Well, then I went on to imagine what the person at the other end would think. The despatcher, I mean. First one driver calls in to say his shipment has been bombed. Then the second. And then the third. And each one also reports an interfering little pick-up appearing from nowhere on an otherwise deserted road.'

'And then?' Sarah seemed to be holding her breath.

'Somebody puts three ones together and gets three-plus. Somebody looks at a map and does some figuring. Somebody sends somebody else – a plural somebody else, with muscles – to find out just what goes on.'

'The next question is,' Kuryakin murmured, 'would they follow the truck route, which would be rather pointless and a delay, or would they be smart and try to intercept us by another route?'

'The question is well put. I have a feeling the answer is about to be supplied free of charge. Far in the distance I see headlights bearing down on us. The first signs of traffic I've seen since we left the last truck!'

The other two peered ahead urgently and saw the far-away eyes coming fast to meet them. Sarah caught her breath.

Kuryakin said, 'If they run true to King Mike's form, they should be large men with shotguns, but I doubt if they'll have anything else on hand at short notice. How long would you say, Napoleon?'

'Fifteen minutes at the outside, by the rate they're travelling. We can pull off the road and let them go by.'

'I doubt if it would work. They must have seen our lights just as we've seen theirs. I'll have to arrange a diversion for them.'

Solo wasted no time in asking what this was. He eased his foot just a shade. 'What do you want us to do?'

'If it is them, as we suspect, better pull up when they say, and keep them guessing for about five minutes. Perhaps Miss Sarah could act drunk. I need only about five minutes. As soon as you hear me yell, get rolling again. I'll pick you up.'

With no more ado he stood, eased himself out of the door of the cab and squirmed away out and over into the back of the truck. Solo drew in a breath to steady himself, and made a tight grin for Sarah.

'You're about to drop your reputation in the mud and walk all over it,' he told her. 'If this is an interception committee from the brewery, then some of them will know you by sight. Do you mind?'

'I'd rather have their scorn than a couple of barrels of buckshot,' she said practically. She peered intently at the staring lights, which were now very close. 'It's them all right. That looks like our local delivery lorry.'

The headlights began to weave in zig-zag fashion across the road so that there could be no doubt they wanted the pick-up to halt. Just to make certain of it there came a double spurt of yellow-red flame, the whispering scream of a shot ricochetting from the road and then the blam-blam of the explosions. Solo trod on the brake, hoping that Illya was clear.

The enemy truck halted some three yards clear on the opposite side of the road, and two large men leaped from the back, each clutching a gun. Lights winked out, the engine died and two more large men scrambled from the cab, also armed. As if they'd rehearsed it, one man marched ahead of the rest, came across and jammed the twin barrels of his shotgun through the side window to within an inch of Solo's nose.

'Hold everything right there!' he commanded. 'I want to have a bit of a talk with you, about some beer consignments.' Then, all at once, his bull-necked super-confidence shivered and broke and his dark-jowled face came close, to peer into the cab over his weapon.

'Holy Mother of Michael!' he breathed. 'It's Miss Sarah, isn't it? What the devil are you doing here?'

'There now, Dan Finnegan!' she complained. 'You've spoiled it, after all the trouble we've taken to be secret about it.'

'About what?'

'Why, Mr. Solo and me. We went the long way round especially so everyone would think we'd gone off to Tipperary or some such place, so that we could sneak back into Limerick and get married. And now you've spoiled it. You'll tell Uncle Mike, won't you?'

'Hold it!' Finnegan protested, furrowing his face. 'What's all this about getting married? It's the first I've heard of it!'

'Me too!' Solo put in, picking up his wits and determined to confuse the issue still further. 'It's all a pack of lies. She was running away from home, and I'm bringing her back. As a matter of fact, I'm glad to see you. She's a bit too much for me, on my own. I could use some—'

'Shut up!' Finnegan emphasized his remark with a jerk of the gun, and then scowled at Sarah. 'If you're getting

74

married' – he struggled to grasp the sense of the tale – 'then why did you come belting into the plant this evening and take something away out of the laboratory? – tell me that! O'Connor saw you with his own eyes. And what did ye do to them beer-trucks?' He got to the main point at last, with a bellow.

Sarah manufactured a hysterical giggle, and Solo's hand began to itch for his gun. The charade couldn't hold up much longer. The other three stalwarts were spread in a ring, all fronting the truck. Where was Illya? he wondered.

All at once the night stillness was shattered by a frantic fusillade of shots, as if half a dozen men had opened up from at least three different spots a few yards to the rear. Solo felt the hair crawl on the back of his neck. This was a good place to be away from, fast. The three sentinels obviously felt the same way. With a silent celerity that spoke of training, they melted briskly into the hedgerows on either side.

The shots kept coming, in ragged profusion. Finnegan cast a worried glance back and around him. Solo wanted no more than that. He grabbed the door handle, slammed it down and kicked the door open, all in one savage movement. The shotgun barrel, trapped in the swinging door, exerted a sudden and painful leverage on Finnegan, jerking him off-balance and against the hood of the truck. Solo squirmed out, grabbed at the barrel and rammed the butt into Finnegan's stomach. The big man, breath gasping from him, folded forward, getting his face square in the way of the butt once more as Solo jerked it up. He went back and down into the road and rolled over.

Solo threw the shotgun away with one hand, drew his pistol with the other, and peered around in the gloom. The gun must have been cocked, because both barrels let go with a double blast as it struck the ground. The distant shots broke out again, furiously, and Solo felt the air around him thicken with flying lead. Then he heard a shrill and raucous yell that seemed to come from somewhere just ahead. He remembered Illya's warning, scrambled up into the truck again, gunned the engine and got the truck rolling. Within

75

yards a dark figure rose out of the night and flung itself at the off-side door.

'Take off,' Kuryakin panted. 'I have no idea what the effective range of a shotgun is, and I'd rather not find out.'

Solo put his foot to the floor and the truck leaped away. Diminishing in the distance he could still hear the running battle of the mysterious armed men from nowhere. He scowled to himself.

'Where did the army come from?' he demanded. 'What did we run into, a private war?'

'Fireworks,' Kuryakin explained laconically. 'Just a lot of big firecrackers – I scattered a few handfuls here and there.'

Solo grinned. 'That's fine, but they won't be fooled for long. They'll be after us.'

'If they do, it will be on foot.' Kuryakin twisted his wrist to study his watch. He seemed to be counting to himself. Then he nodded, and the dark night at their back gave forth a brilliant red-white flare, followed by a sullen echoing boom. 'A limpet-bomb,' he said. 'I stuck it under their hood while they were listening to the fireworks.'

Solo grinned and eased his foot from the accelerator. Sarah stirred.

'I've really torn it up this time.'

'What did you do?' Kuryakin asked curiously.

'Oh, nothing much,' she said, with studied casualness. 'I've only said out loud in the presence of a witness that I intend to marry Mr. Solo here.'

'So?' Solo demanded, feeling uneasy.

'We're very old-fashioned about such things in this country. I'm as good as compromised now, unless we go through with it.'

'Getting married, you mean? Now wait! Whoa! Hold on there!' Solo made instant protest. 'You can't do that to me!'

'I'm not so sure,' Kuryakin murmured contemplatively. 'You could be in bad trouble here. I'm not absolutely certain about the law, but I have heard rumours about it. But I don't see what you have to worry about. I'm sure you will both be very happy!'

'This is crazy!' Solo said. 'One witness, and that was a man with a shotgun pointed at me! They can't make that stick. I'll claim it was under duress. In any case, I denied it. I said it was all a pack of lies. Didn't I?' He appealed to Sarah, who returned him a hurt blue-eyed stare.

'Don't you want to marry me, Napoleon?'

Silence grew and thickened in the crowded cab as he reconsidered his position. Then she could hold her composure no longer and exploded into helpless giggles. He stared, then glared, then looked across her shaking head to where Illya was grinning broadly.

'Two of a kind,' he growled. 'I ought to toss the pair of you out and let you walk!'

They weren't a bit impressed by this threat and Illya turned the subject. 'Speaking of electronics,' he murmured, 'what do you think of this?' He produced his miniature transceiver, which she handled with professional admiration. She was about to comment when the instrument let out a two-tone bleat that was echoed from Solo's pocket. Kuryakin grabbed it from her, but Solo had his out and was thumbing the button.

'Solo here. What?'

'Shamrock to Volga. How are the drains now?'

Solo stared at the thing, but Kuryakin grinned and said, 'Volga to Shamrock. Drains now clear. Some slight obstructions removed, a few interesting developments to follow up.' Solo nodded, catching on. This was the Limerick office.

The small voice came back promptly. 'Cancel developments; stand by for relay from Greatuncle!' The two men tensed, waiting, guessing what was to come. A click, and then Waverly himself.

'Mr. Solo, can you hear me? And Mr. Kuryakin, are you there?'

'Both here, sir, loud and clear. Go ahead.' Solo frowned across at his tow-headed colleague. It would have to be something big to bring the old man out of his lair.

'Good. I am speaking to you from a private charter aircraft; we will land at Shannon within the half-hour. It is first-priority urgent that you meet me there. Well?'

77

'We'll be there!' Solo said crisply, and heard the click of the channel closure. He put his foot down hard on the accelerater, and exchanged grim glances with Kuryakin as the pick-up howled into furious speed. 'The old man sounds worried, and all on account of O'Brien's Beautiful Beer!'

'I think not,' Kuryakin said quietly. 'This will be the second molecule. Meanwhile, what are we to do with you? This party looks as if it is going to get rough.'

'I'm coming!' Sarah declared, very firmly. 'I'm not frightened any more. And if it's something to do with Uncle Mike, then I'm involved. What did you mean about the second molecule? The ferment?'

'Yes. How much of it has been made, do you know?'

'About a hundredweight, I think. It's a fine white powder – looks like starch. The last I saw, it was being put away into plastic canisters, big ones, bright yellow and with an insert in one end. Three of them.'

'I don't like the sound of that.' Kuryakin shook his head sadly, and Solo scowled at him.

'What's on your mind, Illya?'

'Better wait and see what Mr. Waverly has to say.'

They raced on through the silent night, speeding against the ticking hand of time while all around them Ireland slept peacefully in an old-world loveliness of fuchsia hedges and green rolling grasslands, blissfully unaware of the dark seethings of dread that were threatening to plague it.

CHAPTER FOUR

'I'M AFRAID THE BIRDS HAVE FLOWN'

ALEXANDER WAVERLY held court in a small office the airport officials had set aside for his use. His craggy face more worried than usual, an unlit pipe clutched uneasily in his hand, he surveyed the intent faces that waited on his words.

The small room was crowded. As the weary three entered, Solo saw and exchanged nods of recognition with several familiar faces. Enforcement men, and good ones, too. U.N.C.L.E. was showing its muscles. He introduced Sarah, and prepared to listen.

'I'll give you the heart of the matter in very simple words, gentlemen,' Waverly said. 'Dr. Michael O'Rourke has got to be stopped, no matter what the cost, I'd prefer that we get him alive, of course, but if that's not possible—' He let the sentence hang, leaving his audience to draw the implications. His eyes sought out Sarah, peering at her from under shaggy brows. 'This could be unpleasant for you, my dear. If you'd rather not listen . . .?'

'I want to hear it all,' she declared. 'I've nothing to thank Uncle Mike for now. Didn't he try to put me away, and would have killed me as well, if it hadn't been for Mr. Solo and Mr. Kuryakin here? Speak up – say what you have to!'

'Very well. Our technicians have worked out most of the implications of the O'Rourke synthetics. In one form it is a drug which enhances indiscretion and recklessness, depresses caution, and would be exceedingly dangerous if let loose on an unsuspecting population.'

'We've gathered that much,' Solo offered. 'We've had some.' He went on to tell, briefly, what they had done and experienced. 'So we were able to stop the shipment,' he concluded. 'Now we have time to alert the authorities and have 3-B in cans condemned outright. That's a job for the revenue men.'

Waverly nodded. 'Yes. Well done. That will be taken care of. But our present and highly urgent business is to deal with the second form of the synthetic, before it is too late.'

'I don't quite see the danger, sir,' Kuryakin interrupted gently. 'I've seen the formula and read an account of its properties. It's a ferment, a very fast one, increasing in volume extremely rapidly. And it's hydrophilous . . . that is to say, it absorbs water at a furious rate. But—'

'*Salt* water, Mr. Kuryakin. *Sea* water!' Waverly's quiet correction was like a series of ice-pellets into the thick silence. Kuryakin sighed, and then nodded in sudden understanding. For the rest, Waverly went on to explain.

'We tried a few milligrams in a large tank of salt water. Within minutes the whole lot was a fermenting mass, which stopped only because it had used up all the water. And the reaction ends by transforming into a thick jelly-like stuff that is rigid enough to be cut with a knife. The volumetric increase is simply enormous. The simple facts are these: anyone sufficiently familiar with the prevailing tides in this geographical area would have no difficulty whatever in scattering quantities of this stuff – it wouldn't take very much – and thereby blanketing the entire Irish sea, the west coast of England, the English Channel, large reaches of the French coast, and subsequently the North Sea, with this terrible ferment. I don't think I need to spell it out beyond that, do I? Think of the paralysis to shipping, the choked rivers. Power stations would be put out of action, water supplies fouled and cut off. Fish would die by the million from lack of oxygen. And it wouldn't take much of the stuff to effect this.' He paused to study the strained faces watching him, then added, 'We did some rough calculations. All that I have described, and more, could be done with no more than a hundred pounds of the synthetic!'

Sarah caught a hand to her mouth in dismay. 'We have a hundredweight of it already made up!' she cried, and Waverly pulled down his shaggy brows grimly.

'A hundredweight would be more than enough to paralyse Great Britain and a considerable stretch of the French coast. The same quantity again would be enough to eliminate the Balkan peninsula. One ton of it, strategically scattered, would blanket the entire North American continent in strangling jelly-sludge, and I need not spell out for you just what that would do. But it goes even further. Four-fifths of the surface of this Earth of ours is ocean, gentlemen. We all of us depend on it, ultimately, for our very lives. And Dr. Michael O'Rourke has the power to foul the seas of the world, *at will!*'

The litle room was silent as the people assembled there drew their own horrifying mental pictures of what could happen. Mr. Waverly waited long enough for the ideas to sink in, then he sighed and spoke again:

'There it is, gentlemen. Dr. O'Rourke must be stopped, and quickly.'

'It's not going to be easy,' Solo mused aloud. 'That's quite a castle . . . and pretty well staffed. Unless we try to undermine it . . . Illya?'

'It would take too long, and would be too chancy anyway, just to get one man,' said Kuryakin. 'We'll have to siege it frontally. We might be able to dicker, though.'

'Talk 'em into handing King Mike over, you mean? Sarah, how about that?'

'I doubt if it will do any good,' she confessed. 'The Irish are great ones for sticking to a desperate cause. They'd all die rather than give in. At any rate, I know Uncle Mike would. And he's the key one.'

'Are we sure of that?' Waverly demanded, and Kuryakin nodded.

'I heard him tell Trilli as much, myself. Bits and pieces of his discoveries are written down. I have a notebook of his that I took from a safe, and Sarah knows a little. But the basic tricks of the process are known only to him, and committed to memory. He said so. We've got to get him . . . before he can spill it to anybody else.'

'We'll make that final, then.' Waverly sighed. 'We've brought some heavy equipment. Mr. Solo, you're in charge of the direct operation. Take whatever you think you'll need. Stevens, you and Haycraft will go along with Mr. Solo. Peterson, I'd like you to hold back for a while.'

'What are you cooking for him?' Solo demanded.

'I'm trying to arrange for a helicopter; it will take a short while. Peterson can take that, along with whatever forms of persuasion he thinks are advisable, and then he can come in and support your ground attack. You're going to need everything we have. A castle! And it will be dawn in an hour.'

'I think we've thought of everything.' Solo scratched his chin. 'The big thing is to get there fast, before he has time

81

to suspect anything wrong. Where will you be, sir?' he asked Waverly, as the crowd began to filter through the door.

'I shall be at our Limerick office, to pull all the strings I can to get that beer blacklisted. The authorities should be with us that far. I'll take your reports there.'

Less than fifteen minutes later the little pick-up was roaring off again on its furious way. The generator and ultrasonic unit had been cleared from the back to give room for several far more lethal pieces of hardware.

Solo drove intently, thinking ahead, trying to plan a strategy. Kuryakin was quietly busy checking his various pieces of gadgetry. There was just the chance he might have to make another foray up the drain-pipe he had used before. He hoped not, since it would be a bad place to be trapped, but he intended to be as ready as possible.

Sarah sat between them and tried not to shiver. She knew there was a big black car roaring at their heels, and in it two very competent agents, plus some deadly armament. She had no idea what lay ahead, but guessed it was going to be unpleasant. This nightmare went on for a long time, she thought.

'Watch it now, Steve.' Solo spoke warningly into his transceiver. 'We should be in sight of the pile in a minute or two, and they'll see us just as fast as we see them.'

The acknowledgment came promptly. He slid the unit away and squinted ahead in the gloom. The road ran steadily uphill, the only approach, and Cooraclarc commanded the crest. The original builders had chosen well. It was going to be a tough place to force. He saw the grey-black bulk of it now against the skyline, and could reconstruct the details from memory. A massive keep-wall ten feet high and three feet thick. One great gateway in easy view of all the windows. A wide courtyard to cross, under the muzzles of shotguns, and possibly other things as well. The gate came near now: a hundred yards ... less ... it stood invitingly open. It seemed a bit too inviting. A sudden spit of fire came from the top of the crenellated wall of the roof, and then another. A wail-storm of shot screamed off the hood of the truck and hammered on the windshield, followed by a double-bang in the distance.

That had been just a mild foretaste, he thought, as he spun the wheel hard and sent the truck jolting over turf, off the road and in the lee of the wall to the left. He twisted his head around, to see the following car take the hint and roar away to the right. He cut the engine.

'So far,' he said, 'so good. They can't get out. Now let's see if we can persuade them to let us in!'

Kuryakin shoved open the door on his side and slid out into the gloom to circle the truck and pick out a rifle complete with infra-red spotter-scope and spare clip. Sarah was close on his heels.

'What can I do?' she demanded. 'I'm a good shot.'

'You're a very clever girl in many ways,' Kuryakin said, smiling in the gloom. 'You come up here with me.' And he gave her a strong arm to boost her up onto the roof of the cab. 'Keep your head down! Wait just a moment.' He juggled the rifle into readiness and leaned forward to be close to the wall, edging the muzzle up over it. He handed her his handkerchief. 'Now – you just wave that, quickly, above the level of the wall, and then duck. Ready? Now!'

The man on the roof, whoever he was, had sharp eyes. The white had barely fluttered when there came a sharp crack and the scream of a bullet that gouged sparks out of the top of the wall and went wailing away.

'That was no shotgun!' Kuryakin muttered as he pumped three rapid shots into the spot where that flash had been. He thought he heard a strangled howl from up there. Sarah evidently heard it too.

'You hit him!' she cried, waving her hand excitedly. There came another spurt of flame from another spot up there, and the handkerchief was plucked from her fingers. Kuryakin swung savagely, pumped three more shots, and heard the scream and then the impact of a body falling.

'I said keep your head down!' he cried tensely, over his shoulder. 'There were two of them!'

'But you hit the first one!' she protested, stooping to collect the ripped linen and waving it again. He swung back

83

as another flash sent a scream of death close by her cheek, and drove three more shots into that area. Then he drew back and down, grabbed her arm and drew her down too.

'Give me that handkerchief! You'll get yourself killed!' He took the tattered white stuff, draped it over the muzzle of his rifle, and poked it up gingerly. Nothing. He shoved it higher, higher – and there came a crashing blast of fire from the upper windows that whipped the linen away. 'We've cleared the roof, at any rate,' he decided.

Napoleon Solo, meanwhile, was flat on his face by the bottom of the edge of the gate, studying the situation. Intermittent gunfire came from the roof of the black car. He heard Illya's successful attempts to clear the snipers off the roof. He had a bazooka over his shoulder, loaded and ready. Grey light was just getting good enough now for him to be able to make out the darker blotches of windows.

'I think,' he mused, 'that we will start upstairs and work our way down.' He took careful aim; the bazooka coughed and surged forward. The bomb went sloping up on a tail of smoke. There came the crash-tinkle of glass, and then a battering *blam!* as the explosion sent smoke and flames gushing out of the broken window. Almost by recoil there came a stuttering hail of machine-gun fire from a lower window, kicking up the dirt in front of his face and gouging stone-dust from the wall. He scrambled back hastily.

'I see!' he murmured. 'All ready for a siege, are we?' He pulled out his tranceiver and spoke into it to raise Stevens, who was on the other side of the gate. 'They want to make it hard. I think we'd better help them. Grenades and gas-bombs, right?'

He rolled over and stood up in the shelter of the wall, then circled the truck, climbing into the back. He picked up a grenade, tapped Sarah on the ankle to gain her attention and said, 'Watch this carefully. You pull out this pin, you say "Eenie, meeny, miney, mo!" and you throw it – that way!' He winced at the crash from the other side of the wall, and then grinned at her. Kuryakin bobbed up, let off a rapid rattle of fire at the windows and ducked again.

'This is all very spectacular and noisy, Napoleon,' she said soberly, 'but it's not going to get us anywhere. All they have to do is keep down and away from the windows and laugh at us. We don't have anything that can touch walls that thick – not even bazooka bombs will dent them.' The two men stared at each other in the greying light.

'Stalemate!' Solo muttered. 'And with every minute the light improves, it's to their benefit. We might try a bluff. Suppose you talked to them with a bull-horn, Sarah? They know your voice. You can promise them that if they come out with their hands up . . .'

'Wait!' Kuryakin pointed away down the hill and into the grey sky there. 'Maybe this will tip the balance on our side.' They turned and saw the whirling blades of a helicopter slicing the sky.

'That's Peterson!' Solo grinned, and pulled out his transceiver. 'Ground to chopper. Good work, Pete, just in time. It would help a lot if you could lay a nice heavy egg right on – hey! What the blazes is he doing? Pete? Come in, Peterson!'

He stared mystified as the helicopter swung away to one side and then swooped and streaked back in a run almost paralleling the wall. Just above the black car it released a small object which began to drop towards them. Instinctively, the two men ducked into the shelter of the truck, Kuryakin dragging Sarah down with him. The truck lifted and rolled back with the force of the explosion. Solo raised his head and peered at the bomb-crater which had appeared in the ground in front of the gate, then at the helicopter as it went swinging and circling away.

'Whoever's up there,' he said softly, 'is not on our side, that's for sure!'

It had been a long, dreary and dull vigil for Lloyd Gumm and his partner, Louis Addel. Their instructions had been clear and concise: see Miss Sarah O'Rourke safely over to Shannon and home, and then stay at the airport, watch incoming and outgoing flights and make sure she didn't leave again, that none of the O'Rourke brood departed, and that nobody came in to interfere with Dr. Trilli and his operation. When the THRUSH executive gave orders, it was wisest to obey them implicitly. So the bored pair had watched all the flights, all afternoon and in weary shifts, all night.

Gumm was in a snarling mood as Addel shook him out of a snatched slumber, but he stifled his petulance as his partner announced, 'They're here, Lloyd. Big Uncle himself and a squad, in a private plane. They look like this is a showdown! What do we do?'

'We watch and see what they do, stupid!' So they watched and saw the pick-up being loaded, and the black car, then saw them both roar away. 'We ought to chip in,' Gumm declared, not very enthusiastically.

'With what, pop-guns?' Addel said sarcastically.

As they hesitated and deliberated, they saw Peterson approach a uniformed official and they were close enough to overhear him.

'How long before that helicopter will be ready? Time for me to grab a cup of coffee, maybe?' asked Peterson.

'You should just make it, sor. I'll see that you're called as soon as it's ready for you.' As Peterson expressed his thanks and hurried away, Gumm drew his partner to one side.

'That's us,' he said. 'I can fly one of those things. Come on!'

They made their way out to the private corner of the field where a motor coughed into life and great windmill blades began to spin and speed up. Ducking under the downdraft, they ran up to the cab and Addel poked his head in.

'You giving U.N.C.L.E. a ride, mister?'

The pilot turned to grin and nod, and Addel shot him where he sat, before scrambling in, with Gumm on his heels to take over the controls. 'Shove him in the back, out of sight!' he ordered. 'We'll wait a while.'

'What the hell for? Let's get going now!'

'We wait!' Gumm snarled. 'The U.N.C.L.E. guy will be along in a minute, and we want what he's carrying. Now shift that body and shut up!'

The blades whirled into full speed, and now Peterson came, staggering under the weight of two large bags, to duck against the slipstream and come up to the perspex cab side. He hoisted up the bags one at a time, and then climbed in.

'Two of you, eh? All right, maybe I can use the help. Let's go!' And then Addel shot him, dragged him out of the way, took his seat, and the helicopter lifted up and away, swooping swiftly across the wide waters of the Shannon estuary.

In the cold grey of dawn there was no one to notice as two bodies fell into the sleeping water down there.

Solo glared up as the helicopter circled back over its tracks, then he flung himself down and aside as the chattering machine suddenly spat a rain of lead, plucking dust and stones from the ground in a dotted line. A bullet whanged off the front fender of the pick-up. He saw Stevens crumple and go down in a heap, and cursed in helpless rage.

Illya Kuryakin crouched in the back of the truck, his rifle steady on the cab-side, his grey eyes cold. He could just make out figures in that perspex cab above him. He fired, and the helicopter seemed to stagger in mid-air and go sliding away, around and over the castle grounds. He followed it grimly in his sights, saw somebody labouring to stand and throw something. He fired again, and the man fell back.

Then the bucketing machine erupted in a great sheet of red fire and flames, the explosion blasting down into their ears. Shedding burning debris, it fell swiftly, struck the edge of the castle roof, and there was another explosion, twice as violent as the first. And then another, and a blazing ball of wreckage drifted off the edge and fell away out of sight. For a moment they all were stunned and silent. Then Sarah let out a shriek.

'The stables! They'll catch fire! The horses!' She leaped down from the truck and ran heedlessly through the gate, heading for the far end, where the fiery wreck had fallen.

'No use calling her back!' Kuryakin said. 'We'll just have to give her covering fire.' He sprang to the wall, aiming and triggering as fast as he could, sending a hail of lead at the windows which threatened them. Solo came up with the bazooka again and lobbed a bomb into the upper floors. Haycraft, on the roof of the black car, added his fire to Kuryakin's.

All at once the big arched door swung darkly open and a stick appeared, with a grubby white handkerchief on the end of it. The gunfire stopped. Kuryakin peered, caught a stir of movement from the edge of the roof above, cringed as a bullet sent stone-dust into his face, and snapped a shot in reply. He saw Schichi rear up and hang a moment, then fall in a whirl of limp arms and legs, to lie quite still. The stick waved to and fro.

'All right!' Solo shouted. 'Come on out!' He and Kuryakin dropped and ran around to the gate as a dismal file of battered defenders came out into the dawn. Kuryakin glanced away to where Sarah had disappeared.

'I'd better go after her, Napoleon. You can manage here, and she's bound to run into some kind of trouble on her own.'

He ran off hurriedly, around the curve of the wall and into twisting fingers of smoke. He saw her darting and ducking, trying to catch and free a heavy door, coughing as the smoke caught at her breathing. The leaning roof was well alight by now and he heard the horses inside screaming in terror. Dropping his rifle, he put a hand over his face and dashed in, caught the hasp, jerked it free and pulled the door back. She ducked back with him as half a dozen panic-stricken horses galloped madly out.

'There's one more!' she cried. 'Molly! Molly!' He heard the squeal from inside, drew a deep breath and darted in to the choking fumes, to find a bay mare all saddled up and ready but unable to break free. The reins were looped and knotted through a ring-bolt. He jerked them free and drew aside as the mare tossed her head and galloped out.

'Just in time,' he said, coughing as he got out into the open and heard the roof of the stable come down with a crash and shower of sparks. 'Looks as if somebody had that one all ready for a fast getaway.'

'I wonder who it could have been?' she cried as they ran back towards the forecourt, now a scene of confusion. Haycraft stood inside the gate with a rifle levelled while Solo took charge of the prisoners.

He had just snapped a lightweight pair of handcuffs on Foden and Bridget, linking them together, when one of the scared horses took fright at the smoking bomb-crater in the gateway and wheeled away with a flurry of hooves. Foden saw a desperate chance, and took it. Yanking Bridget cruelly almost off her feet, he threw an arm over the prancing horse and swung himself up on its back. She screamed as she was dragged several feet along the ground. Haycraft swore, aimed his rifle, but couldn't get a shot, the other horses milling around in the way. Solo spun and was knocked sprawling by Molly. Foden growled something they couldn't hear, made a mighty effort, and hoisted Bridget up behind him, digging his heels into the horse and galloped off through the gate.

Kuryakin ran up swiftly, to see Solo snatch at Molly's loose reins and swing up into the seat.

'Gimme your rifle, Illya!' he called. 'They won't get far!'

'Bring her back alive if you can, Napoleon. She's almost as valuable as the old man himself!'

'I'll see what I can do!' Solo promised, snatching the rifle and letting Molly have his heels. After a headshake and a kick or two she got the idea, threw up her head and started to run. It took him a moment or two to get back the feel of being in the saddle again, but once he had settled he was in a mood to enjoy the ride. The mare had a sweetly powerful action, and she could travel, too, once she set her mind to it.

'Easy, girl!' he murmured, balancing the rifle across his lap. 'No need to run ourselves into the ground just yet. Let's just see what they plan to do first, shall we? Foden is going to have to do something pretty soon. He can't outrun us with a double load.'

The pair ahead had broken out now on to a wide rolling stretch of green that offered no obstacles and no cover. Solo rode with a wary eye. He had a score to settle with

Foden, and he had no reason to feel affection for Bridget, but he didn't want to shoot an innocent horse. The light was very good now, the sun pushing up over the hills ahead of them in a blaze of golden glory. The soft green under-foot now was too even and smooth to be natural. Solo stared as he realized that he was riding over a golf course.

'I hope the greens committee won't be too upset about all this,' he muttered, and ducked as there came the snap of a pistol-shot from ahead, and then another and the sighing wail of a bullet going by. *Unless he has the luck of the devil,* he thought, *Foden hasn't a prayer of hitting me, with a pistol, at this range, and from the saddle. He must be crazy. The only thing he's likely to do is scare his mount. And it looks like that's just what the fool has done!*

For the galloping horse ahead suddenly threw up its head with a wild squeal and went away at a furious run, heading straight for a low hill. Solo put heels to Molly and she responded at once. Again there came the snap-snap of futile shots. He saw Foden raising his free hand to beat the struggling horse over the head in fury as it thundered up the hill.

'You can't keep that up for long,' Solo muttered, tensing as he put the mare into the first slopes. The riders ahead were black silhouettes against the sunrise, the horse plunging and slowing ... and then stopping, right on the crest. Solo slid down swiftly and rested his rifle across the saddle to take a very careful aim as the horse above swung sideways. He fired, saw Foden jerk rigidly and then fall, and Bridget with him. He went up on Molly urgently, and put her at the slope as fast as she could make it.

The runaway horse stood still, head down and blowing, as he came up to it and stared down the other side. He was just in time to see two tangled bodies rolling over, bumping and jolting the last few feet, to plunge into a smooth green surface that seemed to splash as they hit.

'Hell!' he gasped, realizing what it was. In a flash he was down from the mare and shedding his coat. Frantically he unwound a hundred-foot length of nylon cord from about his waist, snagging the loop of one end over the mare's girth-strap. Like Kuryakin, he had come prepared for just about anything, but his anticipations hadn't included a bog.

Tugging on plastic gloves, he went over the edge and down that steep slope in a mad scramble, paying out the line as he dropped, glancing frantically over his shoulder from time to time, seeing the two inert figures slowly disappearing from sight.

Foden – surely he had hit Foden? Then why was Bridget also so dreadfully still and lifeless? He couldn't have shot both of them! Wild surmises filled his mind as he hopped and slid madly down.

The bottom came close now. Foden was completely under. Bridget lay on top of him, only her head and one shoulder still visible. He let himself dangle, trapped a twist of the cord around one leg, craned perilously down to stretch out a hand and grab, catching at her shoulder, twisting his fingers into the fabric of her dress, heaving hard. He felt stitches parting, but she came up fractionally. He heaved harder, the fine cord biting into his other hand. She came up more. And more.

The stitching of her dress began to part under the strain, all down the back seam. She was slipping out of it, out of his grasp. He shifted his grip frantically and the stuff came away in his hand, wet and limp. He flung it to one side and stretched down to catch her under one armpit, got a savage hold on solid flesh, and heaved until he thought his shoulder-blades were coming apart under the effort. But she came up, and up. He held, caught a breath, made a sudden grab and got her by the waist. This was easier now. A bit more and he could get a loop of the line around her waist, and let go, and climb back up to where he could brace his feet and really heave.

She came up limp in a jackknife position, one arm drawn taut and seeming to be glued into the bilious green stuff. He hauled again and panted. Either he was getting out of shape or she was the heaviest girl he had ever come across. He took a deep breath, set his feet, and heaved until the blood roared in his ears. And then he groaned as he realized what was wrong. Her dangling arm and hand had come clear of the ooze, and there was a slim chain on it. And Foden was on the end of it, down there under the mire.

He skidded recklessly down, digging in his heels, reaching to haul her limp body close so that he could stretch past it. Groping in his pocket, he brought out a tiny thermite bomb and strained, balancing perilously over the mud to jam it in the links of the chain, then teetered back and took the igniter cap in shaking fingers, snapped it into life, and sagged back with a grunt as the thing flared into a moment of searing incandescence, melting the links.

Back up the slope he went, then set his feet once more and with the last of his strength, heaved her up, free of the stinking ooze. He saw her safely settled on a ledge and dropped beside her, to suck in huge breaths and flex his tortured fingers, looking up at the steep slope ahead and wondering how he was going to get her, and himself, up there.

In a while he stood up on unsteady legs and stared at the mare standing at the crest. It was a bare chance. He raised a hand, made a gesture, and called out, 'Go, girl, go!'

The mare whinnied, shook her head, and began to back off, hauling on the line. He stooped hurriedly, grunted as he managed to get Bridget over his shoulder, took up the slack on the line, and shouted again, 'Go! Go!'

Five awful minutes later, dripping with sweat and soaked with the slime that dripped from her, he tottered over the crest and sank to his knees, spilling her on to the grass. She lay quite still, but he had learned, as he had carried her, that she was still alive. He had felt her heart beating as she had dangled like a limp sack over his shoulder. He stared down at her and wiped the sweat from his face. A black bruise on her forehead showed why she was unconscious. She must have got that in the tumble down the slope with Foden. She was a slimy mess, all except her face and one shoulder. She was, he had to admit, a very lovely girl under all that mud.

He sighed, drew off his soiled gloves, tucked them into a pocket, and slapped her face, gently but firmly. She stirred, gave a muffled groan. On impulse he put his head down, slipped his hand under her neck and put his lips firmly on her red mouth in a close kiss.

She stirred, stiffened, and began to struggle, but he held her tight until he could hear her snorting. Then he let go and lifted up and away, watching. Her eyes were open, staring, a bright and beautiful green.

'What – what was that for?' she gasped.

'Let's call it the kiss of life, shall we?'

'But—' She came up on an elbow confused. '—That's for drowning, for someone who—' And then he saw the memory come back to her in a rush as she looked down along her body and saw the slime. She wrenched with sudden terror, her eyes wide, her arms reaching for him, clutching fiercely, shivering with dread. He held her tight.

'Now, now, no need for hysterics. It's all over. It was touch-and-go for a while, and you're a bit of a mess, but you're safe now. Completely safe.'

She made little whimpering sounds, clinging to him, and then she began to weep. He held on, patiently, knowing this discharge of tension was a good sign. In a while her frantic grip eased and she pushed away from him.

'You pulled me out? Saved my life? Why?'

'You ask a silly question like that and you deserve a silly answer, but let's just say I hate to see a beautiful girl going to waste.'

'I'm not very beautiful, right now,' she said dismally.

'I'll tell you better after you've had a bath, but from what I can see, I suspect you'll pass my rather high standards. I'm afraid I tore your dress trying to drag you out. Sorry about that – I don't usually tear the clothes off women, but this was a rather special case.'

She giggled at that, and he watched intently for signs of hysteria, but she had a grip on herself now. 'You're very kind to me,' she said. 'But now you're going to take me back and turn me over to the law, aren't you?'

'Well now,' he said gently, 'you've been a bad girl, you know. You must have known what Uncle Mike was up to, and the THRUSH people. And you were on their side.'

He moved a hand to touch the metal band on her wrist, with its dangling broken links. 'I don't see what else I can do.'

'I suppose you're right,' she said slowly. 'It all seems like a bad dream now, as if it had happened to somebody else. Ever since I was a little girl I've been Uncle Mike's favourite. I always did what he wanted, and he said I was going to be taken care of, right until last night.'

'Then what happened?' Solo asked, suddenly dropping his mildness.

'He and that Dr. Trilli went off by themselves. They left the garrison and the two – Schichi and Foden—' She glanced up to the crest of the hill, remembered what had happened to Foden and shivered, and went on: '—They were to stop back and take care of things. And me. Uncle's last words to Foden were "One screeching female has escaped – you see that this one doesn't do the same. I've no further use for her, but I don't want her running around telling everything she knows!" That's what he said about me, after all these years. But I could see what Foden had in mind, and I was ready to run. That's why I had Molly all saddled up, ready for the first chance I could get!'

Solo could appreciate her feelings at being betrayed, but he was far more concerned by the news of her uncle's flight. He stirred and rose hastily, hauling her to her feet.

'When did your uncle skip with Trilli? What time?'

'About an hour and a half ago. Not long before you came with the guns and bombs.' She spoke dully, her shoulders sagging, but he had no time to waste on her grief. He groped for his transceiver, thumbed it and spoke:

'Emperor to Volga.'

Kuryakin's reply came within seconds, the tone telling its own tale.

'Bad news at this end, Napoleon. Our mad scientist is nowhere to be found. We are rounding up the remains of the garrison and combing through all the rooms. Looks as if the Thrush has flown too.'

'I just pulled Bridget out of the bog and she tells me the same thing. Foden won't bother us again. I'm on my way back. The birds flew about ninety minutes ago, according to her.'

He returned the instrument to his pocket, gestured to her to mount up on Molly, giving her a boost. As soon as he was up after her he set the mare into a steady gallop.

'You could save something for yourself from the shambles,' he suggested, 'if you could come across with a clue of some kind as to where your uncle might have run to. If he has a hideout anywhere, you'd know about it.'

She seemed too stunned by her reverses to be very interested in what he said. He had to nudge her and ask again. Then she craned her head around to stare.

'Where else would he go except the plant?' she demanded, and he could have cursed himself for being thick-headed. Sarah had said the same thing, long ago, that Uncle Mike preferred to meet people at his laboratory in the brewery. He reached for his transceiver once again.

'Emperor to Volga. Illya, are you reporting to Mr. Waverly?'

'I've brought him up to date so far, yes. He's not very happy.'

'I can imagine. He's going to like it less when he hears this. One will get you ten Uncle Mike has gone to ground in the brewery!'

'Yes. You're probably right. That's not so good, is it?'

Solo grinned fiercely at the gentle understatement. From what he'd seen in the dark, the plant was all of a square mile in area, with a high wire fence. And it was daylight now. He could see the castle ahead glowing redly in the dawn sunshine.

Bridget stirred and turned her lovely woebegone face to him. 'Would you give me that kiss-of-life just once more?' she whispered. 'I have the feeling I'm going to need it.

The little pick-up stood outside the castle gates, its engine purring. He slid down from Molly and looked back up at Bridget.

'Go in there and give yourself up,' he instructed. 'You'll be taken care of. Don't worry too much; you've been a big

95

help so far. You can help a lot more by talking, loud and long, to our experts.' Then he slapped the horse's rump and sent her cantering into the gates, muddy and weary. He was rather shaken to see that Sarah was in the truck along with Kuryakin.

'Haven't you had enough danger yet?' he demanded; then, without waiting for her comment, he turned to his colleague. 'What's the situation, Illya?'

'Not very bright, Napoleon. Stephens is able to walk, and Haycraft is unhurt, so the prisoners will be taken care of. But that leaves just the three of us to take the brewery.'

'Three?' Solo shifted his glare back to the girl. 'I don't want to seem offensive, Sarah, but this is no place for you.'

'You can talk!' she retorted. 'You got me into this in the first place, back in New York. You're not getting me out of it now. Besides, I know that plant like the back of my hand. I can help!'

'She's right, Napoleon.' Kuryakin had the truck rolling on its way as they argued. 'She could start by telling us just how many people we can expect to run into. There surely won't be a full staff, at this hour of the morning?'

'No, not until nine. Let's work it out.' She spread the fingers of one hand and ticked them off with the index finger of the other. 'There's two men on the gate, and two men on fence patrol. Four loaders, but we needn't count them, because they've been eliminated already. And two men in the power-house. That's all. Six men!'

'Plus Uncle Mike and Trillie,' Solo added, 'makes eight. Four to one!'

'Since when does three go into eight four times?' she flared; but Kuryakin had a different point of interest.

'Power-house? You generate your own electricity?'

'That's right. Two one hundred kilowatt turbines, one running, one in hand. Almost all our stuff is process-control and a power breakdown would be a disaster. What are you thinking of?'

'I got a brief look at the laboratory in the castle cellar, and it was obvious what a lot of electrical equipment your uncle uses. He will have his own private laboratory at the plant, naturally?'

'Oh yes,' she nodded, and her face tightened as she thought. 'If Uncle has locked himself away in there, we'll have a terrible job to get at him!'

'That's what I thought. He's a man who guards his privacy well.'

'So?' Solo prompted.

'If we can clobber the power-plant and stop all the machinery, *that* will bring him out of his shell faster than anything.' He eased the pick-up to a crawl at the top of the gentle rise that enabled them to look down on the orderly lay-out of the brewery. There was no sign of life or movement. Sarah extended her arm to point, as if the plume of smoke from the tall chimney had not been guide enough.

'That's the power-house. And that building there, that's Uncle's lab.' They went roaring down the road they had travelled once before, and this time they kept on going straight past the main gate, along the ruler-straight road by the fence and to the corner into a right-hand turn. Solo expected his colleague to slow up as they approached the power-house area, but Kuryakin drove on past and then halted.

Casting an eye at the high wire fence, he said. 'You want to bet the telephone has been busy again?'

'The four boyos we met down the road, you mean?' Solo wondered. 'I'd be prepared to believe they've had an interesting story to tell, but I can't see anybody on guard here. Why have we stopped right at this spot?'

'I was looking for a suitably damp patch of ground.'

'Oh!' Solo nodded as if that made sense to him, 'We're going to pelt them with mud-pies?'

'No.' Kuryakin was gravely serious as he slid out from under the wheel. 'We're going to take out their power-plant. Keep your eyes peeled for possible interference, Napoleon; and while you're doing that, have a *good* look at that fence. Don't touch it, just look. Note particularly the insulators!'

Solo blinked, watched his colleague hurry around to the back of the pick-up, cast a sharp glance up and down the deserted road, and then stared at the high-wire fence. Insulators? Given the clue, he noted that the top, second, third and fourth wires were slung from the heavy-angle fence-posts on ceramic holders, and that the wires themselves made unbroken half-loops around each post. Kuryakin came back heavy-footed under a ten-foot length of steel chain that had been used to anchor the generator. Solo scowled at him.

'Electrified fence?'

Sarah made a squeak as she realized the truth for herself. 'I never noticed that before. Now how will we get in?'

Kuryakin dropped the chain and began stamping the shackle-end into a soft muddy patch. 'Your uncle is quite a planner,' he said, 'but this time, I think, he must have been reading too many lurid novels. It's always been surprising to me that in stories and movies when people come face to face with an electrified fence, they get worried. In actual fact, such a fence is a very delicate thing.'

'Delicate?' Solo echoed. 'With several thousand volts streaming through those wires, I'm the one who feels delicate. I'm allergic to the stuff.'

Kuryakin ignored him, pointed a question at Sarah: 'Why have insulators?'

She frowned prettily and said, 'That's to stop the current leaking to earth, of course, through the posts.'

'Exactly. The electricity will run away, given half a chance. I'm going to give it a chance and a half. Keep the engine running, Napoleon; this won't take very long.'

The shackle-end was safely bedded now. He lifted the slack length of the chain and stepped close to the fence, formed loops, made a trial swing, then cast the spare length up and over, and stepped back quickly. The end of the chain cleared the top wire and curled over, flicked back, and for a few exciting seconds even the bright morning sunshine was eclipsed by the corona of coruscating flashes and sparks that spat and crackled where the links met the loaded wires. In the distance, and over the spitting of the electrical discharge, they heard the powerful and quiet hum of the turbo-dynamo lift suddenly into a howl, followed by a protesting whine. The abused circuit-breakers tripped out, the pyro-technics ceased, and the distant dynamo lost its howl ... but by that time Kuryakin was back in the cab of the truck, which was whirling swiftly away from the dead fence in a tight arc, to circle around and drive, full-tilt, to where the two leaves of the fuel-loading gate met.

The three inside ducked and held on. The gate shivered and burst inwards under the impact. The truck rolled forward. As Solo hauled madly on the wheel to bring them around in the direction of the laboratory, they all heard the full-throated roar of escaping steam as the boiler safety-valves lifted.

'That'll keep them busy for a while, Napoleon, so we only have to worry about the fence-patrol and the gate-porters.'

'And to wait until King Mike comes out,' Solo agreed, treading on the brake and skidding the truck to a halt outside the laboratory. To Sarah he tossed the question, 'Is there a back entrance to this establishment?'

'No. This is the only door. Look out, there!'

'I see him!' Even as she yelled and pointed, Solo drew his pistol and fired, half-out of the cab. The large man who had been running urgently towards them along the footpath on the inside of the fence kept right on moving for another six feet or so, but in a face-downwards attitude, and then he lay still, his shotgun skidding away to one side. 'That leaves three, Illya. We're wearing them down.'

The heavy double-doors of the laboratory remained shut. Kuryakin appealed to Sarah: 'What's the lay-out inside, beyond that door?'

'A straight passage, with offices leading off either side, and process-rooms and things. Are you thinking of going in?'

'Better than waiting out here to be picked off. There's a couple of rifles in the back, Napoleon. Discourage the opposition a bit while I go in there and call on Uncle Mike.'

Groping in his pocket for one of U.N.C.L.E.'s special door-openers, the Russian cast a quick glance up and down the little roadway, batted at his blond fringe, dashed across

99

the gap and stuffed the little thermite-bomb in the keyhole, triggered it and dashed back. As soon as the flare had died out he flung himself at the door again, crashing it open with his shoulder and going down head-first in a skid along the polished floor of the interior, his pistol out and swinging in an arc, his eyes flicking nervously in an attempt to watch all directions at once.

The reaction was totally negative. Seconds later the doors crashed open again, to admit Sarah in a similarly headlong dive. As they swung shut after her, he saw she had brought a rifle with her. They lay still and looked at each other for ten heartbeats, then he stirred and got up on his knee.

'The place seems deserted. We'll have to check, but I have a feeling we've missed the boat. Careful how you point that thing!'

With her help, he searched the building rapidly. It was very modern, the sight of the equipment bringing nods of approval from him, but it was quite lifeless. If O'Rourke and Trilli had been here, they had gone again, leaving no trace. Kuryakin sighed and pointed the way back to the entrance, but before they could reach it they heard the *crash-blam* of shotguns and the whipcrack answer of rifle fire.

Orienting swiftly, Kuryakin shoved open a side door, trotted the length of a massive chemistry bench to the far window and peered cautiously out. The next building was some fifteen yards away, and as he looked he saw a jet of smoke spurt out and whip away in the slight breeze and heard the crash of the shot. As Sarah came to nudge his elbow he pointed, grabbed an earthenware jar from the bench and flung it through the glass.

'Keep your eye on our hosts out there while I talk to Mr. Waverly. Maybe he'll have some ideas.' She nodded, settled her elbows on the bench and loosed off a warning shot at the brickwork by the corner opposite. He squatted down on the floor by her feet and pulled out his transceiver, getting Waverly's attention almost immediately.

'We're in the plant laboratory, sir, but I'm afraid the birds have flown . . . if they were ever here, that is.'

'I see. And we've no idea where to look next. A man like O'Rourke might have a thousand hideouts in this county alone, and time is vital.'

'Yes, sir.'

'Illya!' Sarah cried excitedly. 'I've just thought – Uncle Mike's yacht!'

'Eh?' He looked up at her, instantly alert. 'A yacht?'

'Well, that's what he calls it, but it's a thirty-foot cabin-cruiser, actually. The *Princess*, that's her name.'

'Where does he keep it moored, as a rule?'

'It's always in the same place. Regan's Reach. That's a small bit of private pierage just below Thomond Bridge.'

'That's in Limerick?'

'That's right!'

Kuryakin attended to his instrument again. 'Did you get that, sir? About the boat. It's the obvious answer.'

'Yes. If only we'd known earlier. Never mind; we've no time for recriminations. You and Mr. Solo get along to Thomond Bridge as fast as you can. I'll meet you there.'

'Which is all very well,' Kuryakin murmured, as he pocketed his instrument again, 'but there are people outside who don't want us to leave just yet. Keep your eye on the opposition, dear. I'm going to have a word with Napoleon.'

He reached the outer doors, went down cautiously on his chest and drew one of them open to peer out. He saw Solo suddenly bob up from the back of the truck with a rifle, snap off a shot over the cab and then drop again. Hard on the heels of his shot came the crashing retort of a shotgun and the thin wail of flying lead bouncing off the truck.

'Napoleon!' he called. 'There's nobody home. They've gone off in a boat, and we have to get out of here.'

'I'll vote for that,' Solo shouted back, 'but how do you convince the shotgunners over there? There's two of them, and they have a system. One reloads while the other one fires. I don't know where the third character is, but I'm expecting him any time. Do we have any gas grenades? The breeze is in our favour right now.'

'Sorry, I'm all out, but you give me an idea. Keep 'em ducking!'

Kuryakin slid away from the door and went back to the laboratory on the run. Sarah squinted back over her shoulder as he entered, then brought her head back just in time to see a flicker of movement from the other corner of the building opposite. Swinging the rifle, she snapped off a shot and another large man plunged forward into sight, dropping his weapon and losing all further interest in the proceedings. She felt suddenly weak. She had actually shot a man! Then she rallied, twisted her head around again in curiosity.

'What are you going to do now, Illya?' she demanded, seeing him take a couple of reagent bottles from a rack and approach the window to join her.

'Elementary chemistry,' he said, pulling out the two stoppers and bringing them close to each other. Where the invisible vapours met, she saw thick white fumes form instantly.

'Ammonia and hydrochloric acid!'

'Right! Now, give me room to swing.' He hefted a bottle, tapping the stopper firmly into place, swung and threw the bottle through the window and onto the footpath which led past the next building. It struck and shattered very satisfactorily and he repeated the drill with the second, but this one hit and bounced, perversely, without breaking. Scowling, he reached for his pistol, and then ducked as a shower of buckshot stammered about the window. Up again, he took careful aim, fired, and the bottle shattered. As if by magic, a great boiling cloud of white smoke materialized just beyond the far bottle and drifted down to the corner.

'That should do it!' he said crisply. 'Come on, let's get out of here while it lasts.'

Seconds later, with Solo still on guard in the rear, the little truck roared around and away and back through the ruined gate, heading for Limerick. There was a thin sprinkling of traffic on the road by now, so they slowed at the first handy moment to let Solo climb back into the cab, and went on as fast as they could.

Kuryakin relinquished the wheel to Solo and drew out his communicator again, his expression much more serious than usual. Valuable time had been wasted, and if the mad Irishman had in fact taken to the water it might be difficult to follow him effectively. He spoke to Waverly, brought him up to date on events, then listened, and nodded a time or two, made some comments of his own. He didn't seem happy.

'What's the weather report, Illya?' Solo asked, once the conference was complete.

'*Princess* is away. There should be something ready for us by the time we reach the docks. Mr. Waverly's fixing that now.'

'Do you suppose he's going to dump his stuff in the sea?'

'Not here, not yet. The idea seems to be to strike at Britain and France. And that will suit THRUSH fine, of course.'

Solo nodded. It made sense, and from what he remembered of the prevailing sea currents, O'Rourke didn't have too far to go. Once around the southwest tip of the country he would be in the right drift. And that was no more than a hundred and fifty miles. Not far, for a fast cabin-cruiser.

'Is there any way of stopping the damned stuff, Illya?'

'One way, yes. It's mentioned in the notes. If the ferment is caught in its first stages, and smothered with an oily film, it inhibits the whole progress of the reaction.'

'High temperature breaks down the molecular reaction, too,' she added, and Solo snorted.

'Now all we need is some way to bring the whole Irish Sea to a slow boil. That should be simple!'

'I was only trying to help!' she snapped.

CHAPTER FIVE

'TALK ABOUT BURNING YOUR BOATS AFTER YOU!'

WAVERLY waved them to a screeching halt a few yards short of Thomond Bridge approach. His craggy face was grim. He spoke briefly and to the point.

'I've secured a converted Naval motor-launch for you. It's fast, but stripped down completely and devoid of cover. It's fuelled, and with reserve, but you'd better minimize your equipment, to save weight. You may have a long run. I'll describe *Princess* for you—'

'No need!' Sarah interrupted. 'I'm going along with them, and I know that boat like I know my own name!'

'Indeed!' The old man gave her a quick and searching look, then gave her a brief smile. 'Very well, my dear; you should be worth your weight, at that. Off you go then; you've no time to lose!'

They had already planned, roughly, what equipment they would need, and it took only seconds to modify the list and grab the bare essentials. Sarah scampered on ahead, down the cobbled ramp, leaving the men to follow with a rifle each, spare rounds, and the long-range communicator, which Kuryakin hung around his neck. The powerful engines were already rumbling softly as they cast off and dropped into the stern-sheets.

The launch had indeed been stripped down since its Service days. All that remained of the cabin-cockpit super-structure was a three-piece perspex windscreen that served to break the breeze for whoever stood at the wheel – as Sarah stood now, with the throttle by her right hand and her feet planted on a narrow bridge running from one side to the other over the open well where the powerful engine roared. There was a narrow catwalk all around, with a few stout stanchions and a rope-rail to cling to, and nothing else. As she thrust the throttle hard over the launch sat down in the water, lifted her bows to shake off the spray and began to shudder strongly.

'Bumpy ride!' Solo shouted across the whipping breeze to his companion. 'Not my idea of a pleasure cruise!' Kuryakin had his feet on the engine, his rump on the catwalk and one hand hanging onto the rope rail. His straw-blond hair flattened in the wind as he nodded.

'This is only the river. Wait until we get out to sea!'

Solo looked back at the wide wake they were cutting, and felt suddenly very weary, the long hours of ceaseless activity beginning to catch up on him. His thoughts slid into a jumble of confused snatches and highlights. He had always imagined Ireland to be a dream country, all green and quiet and beautiful, a land jogging through history at a placid pace, content to laugh in the sun and take things easy. Perhaps it was. Perhaps he had got the wrong impression. He dredged up odd fragments of beauty. The castle itself. The view over the wide Shannon estuary. Sarah . . .

He looked at her now, squinting into the howling wind. She stood with her feet apart, firmly planted on the boards, her hands holding the wheel, her golden hair streaming back in the breeze. It was hard to believe that she was a laboratory technician and as gadget-crazy as old Illya himself. Tough as whip-cord too, in her own wild way. She was positively enjoying herself now. And Bridget . . . He frowned as he cast his mind back to her. Crooked as sin . . . or simply misled by the overpowering personality of her uncle? There was evidence to show that she was just as clever, in her own way, as the rest of the O'Rourke breed, and it doesn't take much to divert a brilliant mind one way or the other, if you catch it young enough. Perhaps the shock of her uncle's treachery would give her that little push to set her back on on the right road? It would be a pity to see such a lovely girl go to waste.

All at once the launch heaved, leaped, and hit the water with a violent thump. He tightened his grip on the rope rail. Illya had been right about the sea. They were running now in a sharp swell, white foam crests rising and falling on all sides, the launch booming and plunging as it ran up the watery slopes and leaped and crashed back into the hollows. At the high point of each bounding leap they could just catch sight of land, away to port.

'We're passing Kerry Head!' Sarah called, waving. Solo stood up by her side, clinging desperately to rope and windshield.

'You ever done this before?' he demanded, yelling against the wind.

'Not as fast as this. Good job there's not much sea, or we wouldn't be able to keep it up!' She ducked as the bows smacked into a wave and sent a shower of spray whipping over them all.

He squinted ahead and sighed. Not much hope of finding one cabin-cruiser in all this watery waste. But they roared on just the same. In a while she told them they were rounding Blasket Island and heading south across Dingle Bay. Both men were drenched by now, but she was as lively as ever, her face rosily flushed in the breeze. They plunged and surged on, the little launch bucking and rolling in and out of the running wave-crests. All at once she let out a wild hail and pointed forward.

'Tell me what you see, right ahead of us there!'

Solo peered, blinked away a faceful of spray and peered again. It was a long way ahead, just visible as they rode the waves. Black and green, with a yellow trim to the super-structure, and a slim mast with a yellow and green pennant. As he described it she nodded, shaking the hair out of her eyes.

'That's the *Princess* all right, and we're catching up on her!'

The two men braced themselves on either side of her, clutching the frail windshield and staring ahead. The cruiser drew steadily closer. They could see a moving figure now on its upper deck. The view was jumpy as their craft lifted and fell over the running sea.

'Look there!' Kuryakin extended his arm to point. 'They've ditched something over the side. There it goes!'

Solo saw a tiny yellow object bob into view for a moment, then vanish again. He fixed his eye on it. *Yellow*? he queried to himself.

'It's one of those plastic containers with the stuff in it!' he suddenly shouted. 'There! It's floating!'

'What do we do now?' Sarah demanded.

'Head for it. Run up alongside it as close as you can!' He peered frantically around the launch, saw a boathook tucked away down there alongside the engine and dropped down to rake it out. The roaring eased by degrees to a throb and the launch began to wallow and roll heavily as she steered and eased the speed still more. The bobbing yellow thing

106

came close, standing up out of the water like a diseased finger. It bobbed close enough to be reached and edged still closer with the hook. Then Kuryakin leaned hazardously over and seized it, heaved hard, and it came up and inboard. Solo scowled at it.

'Why would they throw it away like that?' he growled.

'Why was it standing up in the water like that?' Illya countered. 'Heavy end down! Let's see!' He hoisted, reversing the canister. And they looked hard. Sarah had spoken of an insert in one end, and there it was. Solo stared, then met his colleague's bleak grey eyes in understanding.

'An explosive charge, and it's ticking away, Illya!'

'Right. We'll have to get it out. Hang on to the canister while I check.'

Solo seized the yellow thing between his knees, then looked up to see Sarah staring down. 'Full speed ahead!' he ordered. 'And if you know any good prayers, this would be the time to try them.'

The engine roared furiously again and Solo felt everything grow fuzzy as the vibration transmitted itself through his backbone, where it was wedged up against the engine casing. He clung tight, watching Illya's head stooped low over the mechanism, watching those clever hands touching and testing, before they seized a firm hold, the shoulders stiffened with effort, and the deadly insert began to move, then spin. Illya rotated it hurriedly. It came right out, a shiny little cylinder of chrome. He clutched it, heaved and sent it in a glittering curve through the air, to splash into the water far back behind the launch. Then he crossed his hands and stared down at the watch on his wrist.

'Seven minutes since they ditched it,' he muttered. They waited, both men staring back to where the thing floated. There came a crash like a hammer blow on the bottom of the launch, a dull boom followed immediately after, and back there the running waves suddenly threw up a spout thirty feet high.

'Ten minute delay switch,' Illya said quietly. 'And they have two more left!'

Solo laid down the yellow canister gently alongside the

107

bellowing engine and stood, taking up the rifle he had put aside. He peered ahead as he came up by Sarah's side. Once again they were coming up fast on the cruiser. He tried to get a firm footing, and raised the rifle.

'If they ditch another,' he told her, 'head straight for it, fast as you can. I'll see if I can discourage that kind of thing, though.' He saw a moving shape on the cruiser, took careful aim, cursing the swaying launch, and fired – once, twice, three times. The moving figure dropped flat.

'There goes the second one!' Illya called, and Sarah began to swing the wheel. Solo hung on, watching the prone figure, then saw it rise and scuttle. He snapped off another two shots but knew that it was worse than hopeless to try and hit anything at this range in such conditions. He put the rifle down and searched the waters for the deadly canister.

'Where is it?' he asked.

'I don't know!' Sarah wailed. 'I've lost it! Over there somewhere!'

They all stared frantically, searching the white-flecked waste with urgent eyes. There it was! She spun the wheel again, the launch heeling hard over to spin about and roar up to it. More urgent prodding and struggling with the boathook as it bobbed close, then again Illya strained over and grabbed, and heaved, and sat with it between his knees, hoisted it over, and began to twist savagely. It resisted his efforts.

'Napoleon! Give me a hand here. They put this one in tight!' Solo stooped and got a grip on it along with Illya. 'Okay? Now – heave!' The stubby black cover gave reluctantly, began to spin. Illya waved him back, rotated it with rapid blows of his palms, pulled it free and threw it, all in one mighty heave. It arched away, hit the water, and the explosion came in the same second as the splash.

Sarah hit the throttle again, and this time both men stood up beside her with rifles, to watch and wait until that cruiser came close enough for a shot. But the desperate men ahead had seen the weak point of their strategy and had taken steps to remedy it.

'There goes the third one,' Solo growled, 'and we'll never

get to it in time! Give it the gun, Sarah – we've got to try!'

He glued his eyes on the bobbing yellow thing in the near distance and counted the ticking seconds in his mind. The launch howled through the water, splashing foam and bouncing from wave to wave. The deadly thing drew close and she checked speed, swinging the stern around in a hard sweep. Kuryakin crouched by the side, glancing from his watch to the canister, tensing himself. The yellow finger waved, surged close, and then the launch heeled in the trough of a wave, tossing him back off-balance. They heard the thing bump against the side – and then there was an almighty *crash*, a shock-wave of sound that nearly deafened them. The launch shuddered and reared up, rolled over and fell soggily back into the heaving water.

Solo, thrown clear by the explosion, caught a breath as he went under, and down, and struggled back to the surface, to blow and stare around, and then strike out for the launch. As he laid hands on it, Sarah's sleek head bobbed up beside him. He hauled himself up, saw Illya's head show on the far side. He turned, extended his arm, heaved Sarah spluttering inboard, and saw Illya scramble hastily to the forward end, to grab and free a gallon can of fuel from its stowage clip. Dazed for the moment, he stared in bewilderment, then caught the idea. The launch was settling by the stern now, and it was an uphill struggle to the bows.

'You take that side!' Illya panted. 'Dribble it out carefully; we can't afford to waste any.' Solo nodded, heaved a can out of its clamps, and leaned over as he unscrewed the cap. There was no need to explain as he saw the surface. For the most part it was blood-red, shot here and there with writhing threads of sickly pink, and it seethed, bubbling and spreading even as he watched it.

He leaned over, his stomach heaving at the sight of it, and sloshed fuel-oil from the can in a thick stream to trap the far edge. The stink of the oil came up strongly, but the stuff seemed to spread and cling to the ferment. He sloshed more over, treating it liberally, coating that evil red-pink stuff, seeing it bubble. A thin finger of it broke away towards the bows and he scrambled hurriedly to douse it.

Snatching a side glance, he saw that the stern of the launch was now under water ... water spotted with patches of furiously-bubbling red. Sarah was up to her chin in it.

'I'm going to duck down and take the top off the fuel tank,' she called, and went under with a swirl of bubbles. He kept on sloshing oil until the can hung empty in his hand and the air was thick with the smell of it. But he had the satisfaction of knowing that the red stuff had ceased to bubble and spread in his vicinity.

Down by the stern were still a few spotty bits, and he started to move that way, halting as there came gulping bubbles; then Sarah bobbed up, blowing like a seal. Around her the oil from below burst out in concentric rings, seizing on the patches of pink as if hungry for them.

He lifted another can and scrambled over to Illya's side to lend him a hand. Five busy minutes later they were able to relax and gather in the up-tilted bows of the stricken launch, surveying the scene. For yards around them the heaving sea was covered with oil-slick, and great masses of lumpy stuff like hideous porridge floated and surged sluggishly in the waves. Bit it was all quite definitely lifeless and still.

'I think we managed to get it all, Napoleon.'

'What about the first two canisters?'

'They seem to be trapped alongside the engine. Safe enough. Not much danger of them bursting, or corroding away. Not polyethylene.'

'That's a relief, anyway. I suppose all we can do now is wait for this damned craft to founder under us?'

'I don't think so. The stern is stove in, and the weight of the engines is dragging that end down, but there should be enough reserve of buoyancy to hold us up.'

'Great! So now we just sit here and wait for that pair on the cabin-cruiser to pick us off at their leisure!'

'It looks like it.' Kuryakin nodded gloomily. 'We've lost our rifles. There's not much we can do about it now.' He turned to Sarah with a wry grin. 'I'm sorry. I'm afraid we got you into this.'

'But you didn't!' she denied valiantly. 'I volunteered!

And anyway, we're not dead yet! Can't we radio for help? You've a radio there!' She indicated the long-range communicator that Kuryakin still had slung on his chest.

'You're not thinking straight, Sarah.' Kuryakin smiled kindly. 'I could call, yes. And help might come, eventually. But we wouldn't be interested by the time it got here.'

Solo smiled wryly and turned away, dragging out his sodden pocket-handkerchief in a futile attempt to wipe the oil traces from his hands. He stared over the heaving billows without seeing them. Help? Yes, Illya was absolutely right. They could call for it, but it would take hours reaching them. And they didn't have hours to spare. At the most, they could anticipate a few more minutes.

His thoughts were curiously mixed. Always, in this hazardous profession of his, one had to face the prospect of sudden death. It was always in the cards. But somehow he had never imagined it would come to him in this way, miles out at sea and helpless.

His fingers met something foreign in the wet folds of the handkerchief, and he looked down. It was a crumpled and wet visiting card, the legend on it barely legible: *Dr. Michael O'Rourke*. He curled his lip at it, took it between his fingers and flicked it away, watching as it fluttered and fell into the thin film of oil. King Mike! And the gentleman himself was just over there, only a few yards away, in his cabin-cruiser. He had been badly thwarted in his maniacal dreams of world-conquest. He would be seeking appropriate vengeance any moment now. Solo sighed, and swung back, to see Illya's face grow suddenly intent with purpose. It was an expression he knew very well indeed.

'What?' he demanded. 'What's hatching in your mind now?'

'Just a thought. Something she said about sending a radio-call for help. It reminded me. That trick circuit.'

The blond Russian dabbed at his fringe suddenly and turned on Sarah in tense interest. 'Let's think again about that circuit your uncle wanted you to design for him. Here!' He struggled to reach into his pocket and get the notebook that was still there, wet and compacted. He shook it briskly

111

free of most of the water, and began leafing through the soaking pages until he found the place he wanted. 'This. Now, what exactly was the idea?'

The two fair heads came close together, peering and muttering, and all at once Kuryakin looked up, blue eyes gleaming.

'Keep an eye on the enemy, Napoleon. I think we may have something!'

The cabin-cruiser had slowed and begun to circle back by now, just in sight from time to time as the waves heaved the stricken launch up and down. Solo watched it, trying to guess which way his enemy's mind would be working. They would be cautious at first, in case they were still armed. But then, by degrees, they would come gradually closer, making sure they were quite helpless. And then out would come their rifles, to make target practice of them.

He felt for his pistol, even though he knew the action was futile. He looked to Illya, wondering what was going on in *that* head, but knowing better than to interrupt the process of thought with time-wasting questions. Sarah seemed to understand him, at any rate, to judge by the way she was nodding vigorously. He took his gaze back to the heaving sea.

The half-scuppered launch was drifting now away from the oil-slick. Not quite clear of it, but almost. And the cabin-cruiser was edging in closer, cautiously. Solo could distinguish two figures standing by the midships guard-rail, staring. One had binoculars. The tall one ... that would be King Mike. Solo pointed his pistol, aiming very high, and fired. The watchers ducked nervously back, but they needn't have worried; they were well out of range.

Kuryakin looked up at the shot. 'Are they that close?'

'Close enough for them, too far for me. How's your department?'

'I think I've got this. It'll take a minute or two more, and some luck.'

Solo saw now that he was tinkering with his personal transceiver, with the cover off, poking at its entrails with a tiny screwdriver. 'You'd better duck down and let us cover

112

you,' he advised. 'They're due to start target practice any time.'

As if they'd heard the cue, the enemy opened fire. Solo could see the pair of them distinctly, O'Rourke standing free with his feet spread and belly to the rail, Trilli more professionally bracing himself against a stanchion, both intently holding rifles. He had heard angry shots wail by many times before but never had he been in such a desperate position as this. The two rifles spoke again, one right after the other. A bullet thunked into the hull of the launch just below them; another screamed from the water no more than a foot to the right. *Getting close*, he thought. And they had all the time in the world to perfect their aim.

'That's that!' Kuryakin lifted his head suddenly. 'If it works!'

'What are you going to do, give them a farewell oration?'

'A farewell message, yes. I've cut out the audio circuits, and shorted some of the resistors. It should give enough power, if only for a brief burst.' Flying steel ripped a long yellow splinter from the woodwork close to his head. He gripped the little instrument tightly. 'It ought to work. Watch those two.'

Three pairs of anxious eyes concentrated on the cabin-cruiser, which was now almost close enough for a pistol shot. The two prominent figures still held weapons, took time about their aim, steadied themselves against the rail.

'*Now!*' Kuryakin muttered, and pressed hard with his thumb on the transmit button.

In that instant they saw the two threatening figures suddenly jerk and stiffen. There was a jet-puff of smoke from O'Rourke's chest, a lesser one from Trilli's. Two muffled explosions sounded, echoing across the water. Then those two men buckled, dropped their weapons, folded like dolls over the rail, hung there a long moment, and then slid and fell into the sea.

'That's the most beautiful double act I ever saw!' Solo gasped. 'What the hell did you do to them, Illya?'

'It was the old visiting card routine, Napoleon. Sarah

113

gave me the clue. Apparently Uncle Mike had an eccentric habit of presenting his visiting card only to very special people.'

'That's right. He gave me one.'

'Well, King Mike isn't the sort of man to do anything without a very good reason. So it was obvious, when I added it to that trick circuit. Those cards are plastic explosive, each one with a trigger-circuit incorporated in it, a radio-frequency circuit. Each circuit is slightly different from the rest, and each one was numbered. King Mike had a special transmitter with a selector-switch, so that he could pick any one and explode it. That's all in the diagram. All I did was to adjust my communicator to a broad band that would blow them all at once, you see?'

'I get it. The old man had a wallet full of them. And Trilli had one. And – hey! Wait a minute! He gave *me* one of those cards, too!' Solo slapped instinctively at his breast-pocket – then, remembering, cast a frantic glance over his shoulder at the oil-slick where he had pitched the card. He saw a great leaping wall of smoky red flame come whooshing across the waves at them as the scattered oil burst into eager blaze.

'Let's get out of here!' he yelled, and flung himself into the sea, the other two only split seconds after him. Imagination made the sea seem hot. For a few frantic seconds they swam as if it were boiling, then they slowed and turned to look back to where the flames were licking around the hulk of the launch.

Solo blew water from his lip and glared at his colleague. 'Just as well I decided to toss that card away, wasn't it? You might have *said* something about what you were up to!'

Kuryakin shrugged in the water. 'It never occurred to me that King Mike would give *you* one of his cards.'

Solo looked back to the burning relic and snorted. 'Talk about burning your boats after you! What do we do *now*?'

'At least,' Kuryakin said, 'the fire will take care of any further hazard from the ferment. It is destroyed by high temperatures.'

114

'I don't exactly thrive on them myself. I suppose we'd better head for the cruiser and thumb a ride.'

They turned together and began swimming for the cabin-cruiser, but they had hardly gone a dozen strokes before they heard an explosive sound which was by now familiar and the water ahead of them was lashed into sudden foam.

Solo snorted again. 'I've never seen anything like it. Irish mothers must give their boy-babies a shotgun in the cradle instead of a rattle.'

'How many would there be in the crew?' Kuryakin asked Sarah.

'Only two – helmsman and deckhand. I've an idea. You two have done all the clever things so far – now it's my turn.' She unfolded her plan, and they didn't care for it at all, but they had nothing better to offer so she won out. 'Don't be too far away, now,' she warned, and set off to swim towards the idling craft with much unnecessary splashing and agitation. The two men watched anxiously, then followed in very quiet pursuit. They saw a brawny figure lean over the stern and take aim. At the very last moment, when they were both expecting to hear the sound of the shot, she lifted her head and began to yell.

'Help! Help! It's me . . . Sarah! They're after me!'

The man in the stern hesitated, leaned forward to peer. Solo muttered, 'She's made it. It's up to us now.'

He inhaled an enormous breath, set his aim on the midships ladder, and went under, swimming strongly in that direction, keeping on until he felt certain the top of his head was coming off. And then, thankfully, he made out the wavering black bulk of the cruiser just ahead. He surfaced, blowing hugely and ready for anything, in time to see Sarah approaching the ladder, and a man on board turning to lower himself a step or two, and to crouch, to extend a hand to help her out. A wave lifted itself between them, went on to hoist her up. She reached for that helping hand, clung to it, struggled on to the bottom rung, then the next, got a good grab on the side-rope, and then, bracing her feet against the side of the cruiser, she surged back and out, heaving with all her weight.

The helpful one yelled as his one-handed grip tore loose, hampered as it was by his ardent desire to retain his shotgun in the same hand. The scene seemed to hang for a moment in slow motion, the helmsman describing an arc over her head, her hand wrenching free of his, then darting out to catch the falling weapon. As he struck the water with a mighty splash, she went up the rest of the ladder like a cat and threw herself flat on the deck.

Solo made for the ladder hurriedly, glanced up to see a familiar double-muzzle aimed at him from over the bows, and dived fast. He came up in time to hear Sarah's weapon speak loudly, saw that the menace from the bows no longer threatened him, grabbed the ladder and went up as fast as he could, across the narrow deck and into the cover of the wheelhouse, where Sarah was busily stuffing fresh shells into the captured weapon.

'You won't need that,' he panted. 'Let me keep him busy with mine.'

'It'll take the pair of us,' she argued. 'He's got plenty of cover up forward, and we've got to keep him busy, to give Illya a chance.'

'All right. You take that side, I'll take this.'

He went down flat once more and edged until he could peer around the wheelhouse superstructure and along the deck. Nothing moved. All at once he heard her let fly thunderously, and two sea-booted feet dropped urgently to the deck up there on his side. He snapped a shot and rolled back hurriedly as a blast of small lead wailed by, bouncing from the woodwork. He waited for the second barrel, and cursed as it failed to come. This fellow was too crafty to fire both barrels at once.

Sarah stood up abruptly and fired blind, over the top of the wheelhouse, and then down. This time there was an immediate reply and Solo chanced his eye around the edge, pistol ready – and then halted, as he saw a wet blond head come up over the bows and grin. Two eager arms reached out, there came a wild and despairing yell, and then a splash.

'And that's it!' Solo straightened up and sighed, feeling suddenly old and tired. 'Talk turkey to those two, will you, while I look for some rope to tie them with.'

Not too long later, with the prisoners safely tied up and the engines growling out their powerful song, Sarah took the wheel. 'Going home,' she said. 'And I do have a home, now. Won't you come and stay a while?'

'That depends.' Solo smiled, as Kuryakin operated the transmitter.

'Volga to Shamrock.'

'Shamrock here. Hold it.'

A click, then Waverly's voice. 'Mr. Kuryakin?'

'Yes, sir. Mission accomplished, ferment destroyed, Royalty and Thrush won't be troubling us any longer. Prisoners taken, no damage to us, threat eliminated. I'm afraid we lost the launch, sir, but we are returning in the cruiser. I would like to suggest some kind of commendation to Miss Sarah O'Rourke, sir. She has been most helpful.'

'I would agree. She seems to be a most intelligent young woman. Let me speak to Mr. Solo, please.'

Illya passed the set across to his companion.

'Solo speaking, sir.'

'Mr. Solo. I have been having a long and very interesting talk with Miss Bridget O'Rourke. She too has proved most helpful. I get the impression that Dr. O'Rourke has been a bad influence in her life.'

'I'm glad you see it that way, sir. I had the same impression.'

'Yes. She tells me you saved her life. Is that so?'

'Well—' Solo hesitated. 'I happened to be handy, that's all.'

'I see. I get the impression that your action has made a great impact on her outlook, that she wishes to reform. I'd no idea you had such a salutary influence on young women.'

A pause, during which Solo frowned, wondering what was

117

coming next. Then: 'She's very intelligent. See what you can do with her, will you?'

Solo stared in amazement at the instrument in his hand. 'What? You mean—'

'There are a number of loose ends to clear up. Damage to the castle will have to be made good, for one thing. And the illegal processes in the brewery must be eliminated and all information we find impounded. A lot to do, and those two girls are the legal inheritors. They stand in need of help, advice and guidance. I'm leaving you in charge for a while. Use your influence!'

'Yes, *sir!*' Solo vowed heartily, and winked at Illya. 'On my own?'

'Mr. Kuryakin will assist you with the technical side. I estimate it will take you at least two weeks to settle everything. I think Miss O'Rourke wishes to speak to you now. Go ahead, my dear.'

'Hello, Napoleon.' Her voice sounded uncertain and timid. 'Did you hear that? Mr. Waverly says you're to stay on a bit and take care of things!'

'That's right.' He deliberately kept his tone casual. 'Help you to make a new, clean start. You *are* clean, I hope?'

'Oh yes.' She managed a laugh. 'I've had a bath. Will you be coming back to the castle right away?'

'Right away.' He glanced at his watch, exchanged a grin with Sarah at the wheel, and added, 'We should be in time for early lunch. Can you cook?'

'Not very well. I suppose I shall have to start learning all the dull things now. No more excitement.'

'Well, now . . .' he said, and raised a brow at Illya's faint grin, 'Excitement comes in several different forms. I wouldn't say the prospect is exactly dull, somehow!'

Sarah laughed, and turned to Illya. 'Dull, he says! Illya . . .' And she paused as if tasting the sound. 'That's a strange name. Have you another one?'

Solo grinned broadly and opened his mouth to say it, but Illya Nickovetch Kuryakin, seeing the terrible prospect of being called 'Nicky' for the next two weeks, levelled his chill grey eyes at his friend and reached for the instrument.

'Napoleon!' he said warningly. 'You too have another name. Would you want me to whisper it to Miss Bridget, right now?'

Napoleon Solo caught himself, closed his mouth hurriedly and smiled. 'I guess you're right, Illya. U.N.C.L.E. agents must preserve *some* secrets!'

UNITED NETWORK COMMAND
FOR LAW AND ENFORCEMENT

THE MAN FROM

REGISTRATION FORM

By filling in this form, you can become a member of
U.N.C.L.E. (United Network Command for Law and
Enforcement) and to receive an U.N.C.L.E. membership
card. Send the form to:

Box No. 666,
9, Arlington Street, London, S.W.1

NAME (Mr., Mrs., Miss) ....
          (BLOCK LETTERS)

ADDRESS ....
          (BLOCK LETTERS)

SIGNATURE ....

A stamped addressed envelope must be sent with each
application.